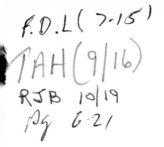

P9-DEZ-104

Blessings
IN DISGUISE

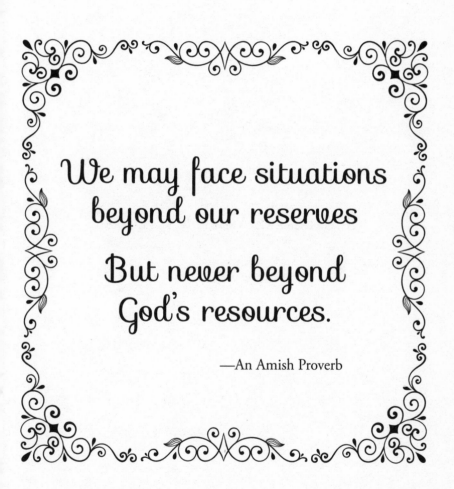

We may face situations
beyond our reserves

But never beyond
God's resources.

—An Amish Proverb

SUGARCREEK AMISH MYSTERIES

Blessings in Disguise

Blessings
IN DISGUISE

NANCY MEHL

Guideposts

New York

Sugarcreek Amish Mysteries is a trademark of Guideposts.

Published by Guideposts Books & Inspirational Media
110 William Street
New York, NY 10038
Guideposts.org

Scripture references are from the following sources: The Holy Bible, King James Version (KJV). The Holy Bible, New International Version®, NIV®. Copyright © 1973, 1978, 1984 by International Bible Society. Used by permission of Zondervan.

Cover and interior design by Müllerhaus
Cover illustration by Bill Bruning, represented by Deborah Wolfe, LTD
Typeset by Aptara, Inc.

Printed and bound in the United States of America
10 9 8 7 6 5 4 3 2 1

Blessings
IN DISGUISE

CHAPTER ONE

Cheryl Cooper sipped her coffee and stared out the window of the quaint cottage. Fall had come to Sugarcreek, Ohio, and the trees were ablaze with color. It was hard to believe how much her life had changed. Leaving her safe and secure job at the bank in Columbus to run a gift shop in Sugarcreek? At first, the idea sounded crazy, but now that she was here, she was filled with a sense of peace. The kind of peace she hadn't felt in a long time.

Her aunt Mitzi had taken off for Papua New Guinea to be a missionary, something she'd wanted to do all her life. "If you'll run my gift shop and send me ten percent to fund my mission work, you can keep everything else you make," she'd said. Somehow, Cheryl found herself agreeing. Even though she'd almost changed her mind a dozen times, here she was. A shopkeeper in a small town hailed as the Little Switzerland of Ohio.

Suddenly, something touched her foot and she shrieked. Looking down, she caught a glimpse of her Siamese cat, Beau, running out of the kitchen. "Sugar and grits," she said under her breath, using a phrase she'd picked up from her Southern-born mother. This game of his was hard on her nerves, but she couldn't help but laugh at him. Ever since they'd moved in, Beau had been busy finding new places to hide. He'd created an odd game in which he jumped out, batted at her with his soft paws, then dashed away like his tail was on fire. Cheryl wasn't exactly sure what precipitated this creative activity, but she assumed he was just excited to have so much room to explore. Her small apartment in Columbus hadn't afforded him much space. She was thrilled he was enjoying himself, but she really wished he'd find a new hobby.

She checked the clock on the wall. It was time to get ready for another day at Mitzi's store, the Swiss Miss Gifts and Sundries Shop. Although Aunt Mitzi's rapid-fire training session had left Cheryl a little shell-shocked, she'd been running the store alone for a little over a week now. She finally felt she was getting the hang of things.

Cheryl quickly downed the last of her coffee and hurried to the bedroom to get dressed. After pulling on her slacks and sweater, she went into the bathroom to put on her makeup and fix her hair. Trying to tame her red hair took a few minutes, but she was finally satisfied with the result. Of course, that didn't mean it would look neat for long. "Your hair fits your personality," her aunt had told her once. "You're too unique to be normal, whatever that is. Color outside the lines, honey. Have some fun!" Well, Cheryl certainly felt unique, but she was pretty certain her definition of that word wasn't the same as her aunt's. And fun? She hadn't had much of that either. She'd waited five years to marry her fiancé, Lance Wilson. Five long years. And then one day he announced that he'd decided he was "not the marrying kind." At thirty, her options were limited. And coming to a small town of a little over two thousand people? Now those options were almost nonexistent.

Something brushed against her leg, and she looked down to see Beau standing next to her. "Have you come to apologize?" she asked.

As if trying to mend fences, he purred contentedly.

She smiled at him. "I love you, and I'm glad you're happy. But if you don't stop scaring me, we're going to have a very serious conversation."

He meowed loudly and rubbed against her leg again.

Cheryl laughed and leaned down to pick him up. "You're something else, you know that?" she said as she nuzzled his soft fur. She gently sat him on the floor. "Well, I'm off. You stay out of trouble, young man, you hear me?"

Beau responded by suddenly racing out of the kitchen like he'd seen a ghost.

Chuckling, Cheryl grabbed a jacket and stepped outside to a brisk fall morning. The October air was invigorating. Since her aunt's charming cottage was only four blocks from the store, she was able to walk to work, something she couldn't do in Columbus. She passed the small general store that sold many of the products produced by Sugarcreek's Amish community. Next to the Sugarcreek Old Amish Store was Yoder's Corner. Run by August and Greta Yoder, it was one of the most popular restaurants in Sugarcreek. Known for their homemade cinnamon rolls as big as plates and tasty sausage they made themselves, the restaurant was always busy.

Across the street, Jacob Hoffman, a Mennonite man who owned Hoffman's Furniture, came out on his front porch, a push broom in his hand. He looked up and smiled as Cheryl walked by. "*Guten morgen*, Cheryl."

"Good morning, Jacob," she called out.

By the time she reached the gift shop, Cheryl was humming. She really did like this town and these people. She unlocked the front door of the Swiss Miss. The store was decorated in the same cottage style as Mitzi's house. The outside was painted a cream color with cornflower blue accents and red shutters. Cheryl particularly loved the turret room on one side of the building, a heart-shaped window on the other side, and the flower boxes under the windows.

As she stepped inside, the aroma of homemade candles, candy, and pungent cheese filled the air. It was a strange mixture, but Cheryl loved it. The shop had gleaming wood floors, a spot in the corner with a potbellied stove, and oak shelves that lined the walls. The shelves were filled with all kinds of homemade gifts and foods. At the back of the shop was a long wooden counter that held an old cash register and several display cases with different kinds of candy. There was a stool where Cheryl could sit while visitors perused the unique items offered. And by the front window was a small table with a checkerboard and two chairs. At first, Cheryl thought it was just for ambiance, but on her second day, two elderly men came in and started a game of checkers.

"How often does this happen?" she'd asked her aunt.

"Ben and Rueben Vogel are brothers," her aunt had explained. "They play at least four times a week. Once in a while, someone else may decide to start a game, but most people in Sugarcreek know it's time to vacate the table when the Vogel brothers show up. They kind of own that spot."

"But they don't," Cheryl had said. "Surely the table should be available to anyone who wants to use it."

Aunt Mitzi had grown silent for several seconds. Finally, she'd said, "Ben and Rueben are rather special. You see, years ago Ben left the Amish church. Rueben was raised to believe that if someone leaves after they've been baptized, they must be shunned. Thankfully, the idea of shunning is slowly fading in many Amish communities. But Rueben just hasn't been able to let it go. If you'll watch them, you'll see that they never speak. They just meet to play checkers."

"Do the leaders in their church support this...shunning?" Cheryl had asked, aghast at the practice.

"Not here," Mitzi had said. "Although the church still takes leaving very seriously, they look more to reconciliation than to judgment." She'd shrugged. "You'll run across some practices you may not agree with. I know it might be hard for you to understand the Amish way of doing things, Cheryl. It's not a lifestyle I would pick, but these are good, hard-working people who truly believe that separating themselves from the world keeps them closer to God. Who are we to tell them they're wrong?"

Although the story of Ben and Rueben troubled her, in the short time Cheryl had spent with some of the Amish people in Sugarcreek, she had developed an affinity for the gentle folks who supplied items for the store. Their desire for a simpler life was something she could understand and appreciate.

Cheryl brought her thoughts back to the present. Even though she was getting the hang of running the shop, she still needed to focus her attention on the task at hand. She didn't have time to daydream.

The bell over the front door rang, and Naomi Miller came in. Naomi and her husband, Seth, were Amish. They provided jellies, jams, candies, baked goods, and different kinds of cheese to the gift shop. Their products were very popular. Not only with tourists but with the townspeople as well.

"Good morning, Naomi," Cheryl said.

"Good morning," Naomi responded. "It is a beautiful day, *ain't so*?"

Cheryl smiled at Naomi's use of the colloquial phrase often used by the Amish. Although Naomi was ten years older than Cheryl, there was something almost childlike about Naomi. An innocence and sweetness that belied her age. She was a petite woman, standing four inches shorter than Cheryl's five-feet, six-inch height.

"It certainly is a lovely day," Cheryl replied.

Naomi carried the basket she was holding up to the counter and sat it in front of Cheryl. "I have apple butter today. And more strawberry jam." She smiled. "Your customers certainly seem to like it, *ja*?"

Aunt Mitzi had warned her niece that Naomi's jams and jellies didn't last long. She'd been right. Especially about the strawberry jam. After seeing how popular it was, Cheryl had taken some home. She'd grown up with jam and jelly bought in a store. Naomi's recipe actually tasted like fresh strawberries, and Cheryl vowed never to buy another jar of jelly from the local grocery store.

"Not just my customers," Cheryl said with a smile. "I'm addicted to it." She grinned. "Two of the last thirty jars we sold were mine."

Naomi laughed. "I am glad you enjoy it, but please do not pay for it." She pulled out two jars from her large basket. "My gift. And let me know when you need more."

Cheryl was touched, but she shook her head. "I can't accept your generous offer. I'm more than willing to pay for what I use."

Naomi frowned at her. "Cheryl, you should never turn down a gift. You stop the hand of *Gott*, and you rob the giver of a blessing."

Cheryl's mouth dropped open. Had she offended Naomi? It wasn't her intention. "I...I'm sorry. It's just that I don't want to take advantage of you."

Humor twinkled in Naomi's dark brown eyes. "My lifestyle may be simple," she said, "but my mind is not. When I offer you a gift, I am aware of my actions."

Naomi's lighthearted, mild rebuke made Cheryl laugh. "Well, your mind may not be simple but mine was." She reached out and took the two jars of jam. "Thank you. This is a wonderful gift, and I appreciate it."

Naomi smiled. "How are things going for you? You seem much more relaxed than you did on your first day here alone."

Cheryl nodded. "I feel so much better. Everything's finally starting to make sense. Not that I don't have a lot to learn."

"You will do wonderfully. We are blessed to have you here. I will miss my friend, Mitzi, but I know she is doing the Lord's work."

A young woman dressed in jeans and a sweatshirt came up to the counter with something in her hands. Naomi saw her and moved over so she could make her purchase. The woman stared at

Naomi for a moment, taking in her modest dress and prayer covering. Then she smiled and held out a cloth doll without a face.

"I love this Amish doll. How much is it?"

Cheryl shook her head. "I have no idea. I don't recall seeing it on my shelves." She looked at Naomi. "Did Aunt Mitzi sell these?"

Naomi frowned. "I do not remember these dolls, but I do not know all of the store's inventory." She smiled at Cheryl. "These dolls sell for twenty dollars at the gift shop down the street."

"Twenty dollars is fine," the woman said as she opened her purse.

Cheryl rang up the purchase then wrapped the doll in tissue paper and put it into a bag. The woman thanked her and walked out of the store.

"That's the fourth item someone has found on my shelves that I didn't know anything about," she told Naomi. "I checked and they're not on my inventory list. I didn't sell the first two things, but I sold the third and put the money in an envelope until I can figure out what to do. I'm assuming my list is wrong. I guess I need to do a new inventory so I know what's going on." She reached down and picked up a large manila envelope under the counter. After opening it, she slid the money inside and made a note about the doll on the outside.

"Mitzi was always very precise and organized," Naomi said. "I find it odd that your information is wrong. What other items were not on your inventory list?"

"A woven basket, a carved wooden horse, and a cross-stitched dish towel." She picked up the horse and the towel from a shelf under the counter and put them on the glass countertop. "They're beautifully made, but I don't feel right selling them. I have no idea where the money is supposed to go."

"Maybe someone is trying to bless you," Naomi said gently. "I would not worry about it."

"Maybe," Cheryl said slowly.

A man came up to the women with a Bible in his hands. "I'm sorry. I didn't see a price tag anywhere."

A King James Version Bible was tucked into a beautiful hand-tooled leather cover. Cheryl shot Naomi a look. "I'm sorry, sir," she said. "Where did you find this?"

The man motioned over to a shelf near the front door. "It was there, next to the wooden birdhouses."

"I think someone left it here by mistake," Cheryl said. "I'm terribly sorry, but I can't sell it to you."

The man shook his head. "That's too bad." He ran his hand over the cover. "This work is exceptional."

"Yes, it is," she agreed. "Again, I apologize."

"Not a problem," he said with a smile. "I wouldn't want to make off with someone else's Bible." He put it on the counter. "I own a hardware store in Oklahoma. My advice to you is to find out who made this cover and acquire some for your shop. I guarantee you they'll sell."

Cheryl thanked him, and the man left to join a woman who was looking at jars of apple butter.

"See," she whispered to Naomi. "That's what I'm talking about. Something really strange is going on."

She picked up the Bible so she could put it on the shelf behind the counter with the wooden horse and the towel. As she leaned over, a piece of paper fell out from between the pages. Cheryl picked it up and read:

You need to be very careful. Someone in Sugarcreek is not who they say they are!

Chapter Two

Cheryl handed the strange note to Naomi who read it slowly, a troubled look on her face. When she gave it back, Cheryl noticed she'd grown pale.

"I wouldn't take it too seriously, Naomi. We have no idea what it means or who wrote it. It might even be a joke."

"*Ach*, you do not understand," Naomi said quietly. "The Bible. It belongs to our son, Levi. I was starting to tell you when the note fell out."

Cheryl placed the Bible back on the counter. "But why was it on one of my shelves?"

Naomi shook her head. "I do not know. Levi dropped off a batch of fudge Saturday afternoon, ja? Maybe he accidentally left his Bible behind." She frowned and pointed to the note lying on the counter. "But this is not Levi's writing."

Cheryl frowned. "That's odd." She pushed the Bible toward Naomi. "Why don't you take this back to Levi and ask him about the note? Maybe he has an explanation. I'm sure it's nothing to worry about."

Naomi nodded slowly. "I am sure you are right."

Cheryl lightly touched the tooled leather book cover that protected the Bible. Flowers and vines, done in intricate scrollwork, surrounded a finely detailed cross. It was breathtaking. "This is the most beautiful cover I've ever seen, Naomi. May I ask where Levi got it?"

Naomi's apprehensive expression melted. "Levi made this himself," she said, a touch of satisfaction in her voice. "Gott is good. He gave our Levi the skill of a craftsman."

Cheryl smiled. Naomi always said positive things about her children, but she consistently gave the honor for their accomplishments to her "Gott." The older children, Levi, Caleb, and Sarah, were born to Ruth, Seth's first wife who died in childbirth. Siblings Eli, Elizabeth, and Esther were the couple's biological children. However, in Naomi's heart there was no difference in the love she generously bestowed on each of them without a hint of favoritism. To Naomi, they were all her children. The only child she never mentioned was Sarah, the daughter whose birth cost Ruth Miller her life. Aunt Mitzi had explained to Cheryl that following a period of *rumspringa*, an Amish tradition considered a rite of passage, Sarah left Sugarcreek and married an *Englischer*. She and her husband, Joe, now lived in nearby Canton, but ties between her and her parents had been broken. Seth and Naomi weren't even invited to Sarah's wedding.

Although Cheryl tried to understand rumspringa, she had a hard time with it. Supposedly, it was a time in the life of an Amish youth when they were given the choice to become part of the Amish church or leave their community and live in the world. Rules and restrictions were relaxed, but unfortunately, some teenagers went off the rails. Drinking, smoking, and even wild parties were tolerated by parents praying their children would decide to turn their backs on the world and embrace the faith they'd been raised in. Cheryl couldn't make sense of giving a child permission to partake in activities that could harm them, hoping they'd choose the right way.

"Perhaps it's not our way," Mitzi had told her, "but the idea is to make certain the young person follows God based on his or her own decision. I'm afraid there are many in our churches who call themselves Christians because they were raised in the church, yet they've never made a personal commitment to Christ. Their roots aren't deep. When tribulation comes, they fall away." She'd smiled at her niece. "God doesn't want us to serve Him out of tradition, honey. He wants us to follow Him because we choose to. Do you understand?"

Her aunt's explanation helped, but Cheryl still had a problem with the concept of rumspringa. If she'd asked her parents for the chance to act wild for a while to see if she wanted to do the things they'd taught her, she would have spent the next few months grounded to her room. She missed her parents who lived in Seattle. Her father was the pastor of a large church, and Cheryl didn't get to see them as much as she'd like.

Cheryl realized that her mind had wandered, and she refocused her attention on the beautiful Bible cover. "Do you think Levi would be interested in making some of these for me?" she asked. "I think I could easily sell them in the store."

Although Aunt Mitzi had given Cheryl carte blanche to add items to the store's inventory, this was the first time she'd actually attempted to stock a new product. Excited about the exquisitely made covers, she waited with anticipation for Naomi's response.

"Your aunt asked Levi the same thing," Naomi said, "but he refused her. He is very busy with our farm. As you know, besides taking care of our crops and cattle, we have a petting zoo and a corn maze. Occasionally we also offer buggy and hayrides. The girls help me with the goods I bring to you, but my boys and Seth spend long days keeping up with the farm and our activities."

Cheryl nodded, even though she hadn't received the response she'd hoped for. "I understand. If he should ever find the time, the offer stands." She smiled at her Amish friend. "You and your family have certainly been blessed with creativity."

Naomi shyly returned Cheryl's smile. "Gott is good," she said again.

Cheryl took the basket of jams and jellies, then she removed an envelope from under the tray in the cash register and handed it to Naomi. "Here are the proceeds from your last batch of goodies. I can't keep your banana bread on the shelf, and we have standing orders for cream cheese and aged sharp cheddar."

Naomi wrinkled her nose and laughed lightly. "Some of your customers do not understand what the term *aged* means, ain't so?"

Cheryl grinned at her. "That's definitely true."

Naomi put the envelope Cheryl had given her into the pocket of an apron she wore over her simple blue dress. Then she picked up Levi's Bible, said good-bye, and left.

It was a busy morning. Cheryl was just wrapping up a jar of apple butter when a woman came up to the counter. She waited until Cheryl was free and then put a beautifully embroidered dresser scarf on the counter. The ends were decorated with large blue hearts. Inside each heart was a red flower with green leaves.

Cheryl sighed. "Can I ask where you found this?"

The woman pointed toward the shelves that held quilted oven mitts and aprons. "It was folded up and stuck under your aprons, but there's no price on it."

Thinking quickly, Cheryl said, "How does thirty dollars sound?"

The woman smiled. "That sounds perfect. It's just lovely. My grandmother used to do embroidery like this."

While the woman shuffled through her purse for the money, Cheryl made another note on the envelope she kept under the counter. The list of mysterious items was growing. She glanced around the store to see if there was anyone who didn't look like they belonged, but no one seemed suspicious. Of course, the table scarf could have been put there several days ago without Cheryl's knowledge. It seemed that someone had purposely tried to hide it.

A little before noon, Naomi's daughter, Esther, walked through the front door. She worked three hours a day while Cheryl had lunch and worked on the books in the small office tucked away in the back. Esther was a sweet girl who reminded Cheryl of a young Naomi. She was reluctantly participating in rumspringa, encouraged by her friend, Lydia Troyer. After what happened to Sarah, Naomi was obviously concerned about the situation although she'd only mentioned it briefly to Cheryl. And Lydia, who also helped out in the store from time to time, wasn't doing anything to quell Naomi's fears. Lydia seemed to embrace the idea of the unusual practice.

After bringing Esther up-to-date on the morning, Cheryl decided to ask her about the strange items showing up on her shelves.

"I'm sorry, I haven't noticed anything," Esther said, her perfect, delicate features marred by a frown.

"Okay. If a customer brings something up to the register that we don't carry—or if it doesn't have a price tag, will you let me know?"

She nodded. "Ja, I will." She took an apron from beneath the counter and slipped it on over her plain dress. Naomi had made special aprons for the employees of the Swiss Miss. Red, with white hearts appliquéd on the bib, and the words *The Swiss Miss* stitched inside the heart. The heart was chosen because of the store's heart-shaped window. There were two pockets with the same heart on the pockets. Cheryl loved the special aprons. Not only because of how cute they were, but also because the large pockets were so handy. After bringing the ties around front and securing the apron, Esther shook her head. "I cannot understand why anyone would place these things in the shop. They would not receive payment. It does not make sense."

Cheryl smiled at the dark-haired girl. "No, it doesn't, does it? It's a mystery." She glanced at her watch. "I'm going to run across the street to the Honey Bee Café. I'm craving one of their bacon, apple, and cheddar grilled cheese sandwiches." The Honey Bee's different varieties of grilled cheese sandwiches were a favorite among local residents. Cheryl had tried several varieties and thought each selection was fabulous.

Esther smiled. "They are delicious, ain't so?"

Cheryl sighed. "They're addictive. But everything at the Honey Bee is wonderful." She had half a mind to end her sentence with, "ain't so," but she didn't. The last thing she wanted was for Esther to think she was mocking her.

She grabbed her coat and scooted out the front door. It only took a minute to get across the street to the café. The old building had housed several businesses, most recently a craft store. It had been completely renovated and was one of the most popular places to eat in Sugarcreek. The Honey Bee served fresh foods such as sandwiches, soups, salads, and baked goods, as well as specialty coffees, teas, hot chocolate, and smoothies. The owner, Kathy Snyder, was committed to serving several healthy items along with the wonderful desserts that Cheryl found herself craving. Painted a beautiful dark gray with white accents, the building had a huge front porch with several small tables and chairs. When the weather was nippy, as it was today, Cheryl liked to sit there and have lunch. Something about the fall weather invigorated her.

Next door to the café was the Bye Bye Blue Art Studio. When she had time, Cheryl loved to check out the new paintings and artwork in the store. She hoped to pop in after lunch so she could see what new items were on display.

She went inside and ordered the special grilled cheese sandwich, along with a pumpkin spice latte. Then she checked the porch and was pleased to find an empty table. While she waited for her lunch, she gazed around at the bustling shops on Main Street. To her, the Swiss Miss was the most beautiful building in downtown Sugarcreek, but she also loved the other unique businesses that lined the street. A feeling of peace washed through her. Sugarcreek was certainly different than Columbus, but she wasn't the least bit homesick. In fact, Sugarcreek felt more like home than anyplace she'd ever been. Funny how God could take the worst time of her life and turn it around.

"Thank You, God," she whispered.

A few minutes later the front door of the café opened and one of the waitresses brought out her lunch. As Cheryl thanked her, the door opened again and Bob Gleason and his wife, Tillie, came out. They owned Amazin' Corn, the corn maze next door to the Swiss Miss.

"Why, hello there," Bob bellowed. His loud voice made the waitress jump. She nodded at Cheryl and hurried back inside.

"Hello," Cheryl replied, hoping they wouldn't try to join her for lunch. She liked the couple. They'd been friendly and welcoming, but they seemed a little overly enthusiastic about everything, and Cheryl found it a little disconcerting.

"Do you eat here often?" Tillie asked.

Cheryl nodded at the overly made-up middle-aged woman with poofy blonde hair and jeweled eyeglasses. Tillie was a buxom woman who dressed like a teenager. Tight black leggings showed off her chubby legs, and an equally snug purple sweater with gold sequins clearly outlined what Aunt Mitzi referred to as "love handles." Actually, underneath the loud makeup and poor clothing choices, Cheryl could see that Tillie was a pretty woman.

Like his wife, Bob was also over-the-top. A tall man with a big belly, he dressed as if he thought Sugarcreek had been plopped down in the middle of a Western movie. Cowboy boots, jeans, Western shirts, and a huge Stetson made him look more like a cattle rancher in Texas than a business owner in Sugarcreek, Ohio.

"Grilled cheese, huh?" Bob said, staring at Cheryl's plate. "Wish I'd gotten that. Had a burger instead. It was great, but I sure love their grilled cheese too."

Cheryl had the weirdest feeling Bob was waiting for her to offer her lunch to him, but she dismissed it as her imagination.

"Have you tried their oatmeal walnut chocolate chip cookies?" Tillie purred. She looked skyward as if the cookies were somehow sent directly from above. "I just can't get enough of them." She patted the roll of fat along her waist. "I swear, if I didn't eat so many I'd be skinny as a rail."

Bob snorted and put his arm around her. "I don't want no skinny woman, honey bun. I like my woman to have a little meat on her. Makes you easier to hug."

Tillie giggled. "Oh, Bob. You're gonna embarrass Cheryl. Stop it now."

Cheryl forced herself to smile. "No, not at all."

"When are you goin' through our maze?" Tillie asked in a whiny voice. "We keep askin' you, but you still haven't come by."

"I'm sorry," Cheryl said. "I've been really busy trying to learn how to run my aunt's store. I'm sure you understand."

Tillie stuck out her bottom lip. "It don't take long." She opened her glittery gold purse and reached inside. "Here's a free ticket. You just give it to Stanley. He's watchin' the entrance this afternoon. Bob and I gotta run over to the bank for a while, but Stanley will help you."

Cheryl took the ticket Tillie stuck in her face. "Thank you. Maybe after I finish my lunch—"

"That's it," Bob said jovially. "You stop by on your way back to work. You'll love it. And if you get lost, you yell for Stanley. He'll come find you."

Tillie nodded. "Stanley is Bob's . . . brother."

The couple exchanged a quick look between them, leaving Cheryl to wonder what was up with Stanley.

"I will," she said finally, trying to get the Gleasons to leave so she could finish her sandwich. Seemingly satisfied, they said good-bye and headed across the street to Amazin' Corn. Cheryl watched as they jumped into their Cadillac and drove away.

She really wasn't that excited about going through the maze, but she had to admit she was a little curious about it. Since the Millers also had a corn maze at their farm, this was a chance to compare the two. Besides, if she went to the corn maze while the Gleasons were gone, maybe she could hurry through without them tagging along. Reluctantly, she decided to put off her visit to Bye Bye Blue for another time. Before she left, Cheryl went back inside the restaurant and, giving in to temptation, she ordered a dozen oatmeal walnut chocolate chip cookies—to share, of course. The girl at the counter said they would be ready the next morning and could be picked up at any time.

Ten minutes later, Cheryl stood at the entrance to Amazin' Corn, reading a crudely drawn sign Enter at Your Own Risk. Not Responsible for Accidents. There was a table and a chair sitting there, but the chair was empty. She checked around but wasn't able to scare up anyone. No one taking tickets, no visitors, and no Stanley.

Finally, she put her ticket into the box on the edge of the table and stepped inside. Might as well get it over with. At least she'd be able to tell Bob and Tillie she'd gone through their maze.

A moldy, musty smell assailed her nose as soon as she entered. Various cheap decorations were tied to corn stalks. Plastic crows and artificial fall flowers discolored by the sun were the most prevalent. As Cheryl took a left turn, she came upon a hay bale sitting in the corner. An old scarecrow sat forlornly on top, his clothes falling apart and his painted smile faded with age.

Cheryl had just walked around a turn at the back of the maze when she heard a phone ring. Then a man's voice. She couldn't see him, but she could hear him clearly. She froze in place when she heard him say, "No, I haven't found her yet, Arch," he said in a deep voice that sounded more like a snarl. "But I will. And when I do, I'm going to kill her."

CHAPTER THREE

Horrified by what she'd heard, Cheryl began to hurry through the maze, trying to locate the way out, but she couldn't find the exit. Turn after turn led her nowhere. Finally, out of frustration, she pushed through the corn, breaking some of the stalks. She felt one of the damaged stalks scrape her ankle, and she cried out in pain. Not taking time to see how badly she was injured, she quickly looked around, trying to get her bearings. She was on the far side of the maze, not as close to the Swiss Miss as she'd hoped. Not knowing what else to do, she hurriedly walked toward the sidewalk, joining a group of tourists taking pictures of the quaint downtown area. Although she glanced back toward the maze several times, she didn't see anyone else coming out.

When the group reached the sidewalk in front of the Swiss Miss, Cheryl broke away and limped toward her store, trying to keep an even pace so as not to draw too much attention. As she entered the shop, she found Esther talking to a customer about the different kinds of Amish cheeses kept in the store's small cooler. When she noticed Cheryl, her eyes widened with alarm.

"Are you all right?" she asked.

Cheryl, embarrassed by her unkempt appearance, nodded and made a beeline for her office. Her hair had caught on some of the corn stalks as she ran out, and her coat was dirty. Even though she couldn't see herself, she was certain she looked a sight. Thankfully, there was a small half-bathroom connected to the office where she could clean up. As soon as she closed the bathroom door, she noticed blood on her shoe. She washed her face and ran her hands through her hair, trying to dislodge pieces of corn stalk. Then she grabbed some paper towels, ran one of them under the water, and went back into her office. She'd just taken off her coat and had plopped down in her chair when the door to her office swung open and Esther came in.

"Ach, you have hurt yourself, Cheryl. What happened?"

"I...I went through the corn maze next door and cut myself on a broken stalk." She pulled up her pant leg, and the women stared at a pretty good-sized gash on her ankle.

Esther came over and gently took the paper towels from her employer. Then she knelt down next to Cheryl and carefully cleaned the wound. "Do you have any antiseptic?" she asked.

"There's some hydrogen peroxide under the sink," she said. "Aunt Mitzi told me to always keep some handy in case someone needed it."

While Esther went back to get the peroxide, Cheryl tried to figure out what to do next. She was beginning to wonder if the man in the maze was really serious. A lot of people used the phrase, "I'm going to kill you," but they didn't mean they were actually going to murder someone. What if she contacted the police and it was just an offhand, careless remark? Had she overreacted?

"Here we go," Esther said as she stepped back into the room. "Your aunt is a very wise woman, ja? She has provided everything we need to tend to your injury."

Cheryl managed a weak smile. "Yes, she is wise. Sometimes I feel she's still here, watching over me. I'll need something, and it will suddenly show up."

"Gott provides through those who love us, ain't so?"

She nodded. "Yes, He does." She took a deep breath. "Esther, I'm afraid I caused some damage to the Gleasons' maze. I may have ruined some of their stalks."

"*Pffft*," the girl replied. "I would not worry about that. Mr. Gleason will probably just pick up the broken pieces and tie them to stakes. He does not take very good care of his maze."

Cheryl looked at her in surprise. It was the first time she'd heard Esther say anything even vaguely negative about another person.

Esther caught Cheryl looking at her, and she blushed. "I am sorry," she said softly. "I should not have spoken so."

"I'm sure you didn't say anything that isn't true."

"That may be, but it is not my place to judge." She put a large bandage on Cheryl's cut and then stood up. "You must come to our farm and visit our maze. You will find it very different."

"I appreciate the offer," Cheryl said slowly, "but I got a little panicked. Maybe corn mazes aren't for me."

Esther frowned at her. "Why would you panic in a maze? Your map should show you the way out."

"Map? I didn't have a map."

She sighed. "You should have been given a map. A corn maze should be fun, not frightening."

Cheryl explained to her that no one was there when she entered. "There may have been maps at the entrance. I just didn't see them."

"Or perhaps it was too much trouble to..." She stomped her foot and sighed dramatically. "There I go again. Maybe rumspringa is having a bad effect on me."

Cheryl pulled her pant leg down. Her ankle hurt and felt stiff. "If you don't want to be involved in...rumspringa, Esther, why not withdraw?"

Esther looked away for a moment before saying, "Lydia tells me I should be certain about being baptized into the church. I do not want to make a mistake."

Cheryl remembered a question Aunt Mitzi had asked her more than once. "What does your heart tell you, Esther?"

Esther's dark brown eyes filled with tears. "I love my life," she said. "And my family. I am not saying other ways of living are wrong, but I do not think I want a life away from what I know. It is very hard..."

Cheryl reached out and took the girl's hand. "I believe you'll make the right choice when the time comes. Follow God, Esther. And don't let Lydia talk you into something that isn't right for you."

"We have been best friends since we were little girls. I do not want to lose her."

Cheryl squeezed Esther's hand and let it go. "Be honest with her. Tell her you have doubts. You may find she's feeling exactly the way you do." She smiled at Esther. "I'm sure Lydia doesn't want to lose you either."

Esther wiped away a tear that snaked down her cheek. "Your words make good sense." She gave Cheryl a quick hug. "Thank you so much."

The bell over the front door rang. Esther wiped her face with her apron and hurried out front to greet whoever had entered. Cheryl sat back down in her chair, still thinking about the incident in the maze while trying to concentrate on the paperwork that awaited her.

About an hour later, Esther informed her that a tour bus had pulled up across the street and was unloading passengers intent on exploring the wonders of Sugarcreek. When the buses showed up, things got very busy as scores of excited tourists invaded the downtown stores. Many of the bus riders headed to the Swiss Miss while some of them made a beeline to the Sugarcreek Sisters Quilt Shoppe next door. A few older women went straight to the fruit and produce stand set up in front of the Christian bookstore. Fall apples and pears were a hit, but the big sellers right now were okra and pumpkins. Cheryl watched as the women bought large bags full of organic fruits and vegetables. When they had all they could carry, they lugged their treasures over to the bus driver who stowed them away so the women could continue their shopping.

Cheryl noticed the bus driver with Annie's Amish Tours wasn't the same one she'd seen before and wondered if he was new or just filling in. After securing the women's bounty in a large compartment on the side of the bus, he leaned against the bus and lit a cigarette. Cheryl had the strangest feeling he was watching the store, and it gave her an uneasy feeling. She became too busy to pay any attention to him as she helped customers with their purchases. Cheryl sold all the jams and jellies Naomi had just delivered. Eventually, customers thinned and the bus took off for the next exciting spot on their tour. As they drove away, a buggy pulled up outside the front door, and Cheryl watched as Naomi climbed down.

"Is it three o'clock already?" Cheryl said, looking at her watch. The afternoon had flown by.

"Ja, it does not feel that late to me either," Esther said. She quickly began to straighten some of the shelves left in disarray by careless customers who didn't bother to put items back neatly after looking at them. Cheryl walked over to the door and greeted Naomi as she came inside.

"Levi is busy at the farm, so I came to pick Esther up," she said to Cheryl.

"I'm glad you're here. Can I talk to you for a minute?"

"Of course," Naomi said with a gracious smile.

"Esther, will you work just a little longer while I talk to your mother?"

"Ja, I would be happy to."

Cheryl motioned to Naomi to follow her into the office. Once both the women were inside, Cheryl closed the door. She pointed at a chair in front of her desk. "Have a seat. I'll try not to keep you too long."

Naomi shook her head. "I have time for you. Do not worry." Her smile slipped a little. "I hope you are not having problems with Esther?"

Cheryl shook her head as she sat down in her desk chair. "Oh my goodness, no. She's wonderful. That's not it at all."

"Then what can I do for you?"

Cheryl took a deep breath. "I need your advice. Something… happened." She proceeded to tell Naomi about the incident in the maze. By the time she finished, Naomi had a troubled look on her face.

"So someone's life has been threatened? Should you not contact the police?"

"I'm just not sure. I know you would never make a comment like the one I mentioned, but people in the world sometimes use it as a way to express frustration. It doesn't mean they really intend to kill anyone. I'm new in Sugarcreek, Naomi. If I contact the police chief and turn out to be wrong…"

Naomi's expression made it clear the man's words had stunned her gentle, loving sensibilities. Finally, she shook her head. "It is difficult to understand the ways of the world sometimes, but I am certain you will make the right decision."

Cheryl smiled at her Amish friend. "Thank you for listening. It's nice to have someone to talk to."

Naomi nodded slowly. "You know, when I first got to know your aunt, I did not believe I could ever be…close to an Englischer. Do not misunderstand. We have contact with many in our community who do not believe the way we do. But these relationships come from activities at our farm—or from the sale of our products. However, your aunt showed me that people who love Gott are not so different. To my surprise, Mitzi became…my dear friend." She smiled at Cheryl. "And I hope we will become friends as well."

Cheryl returned the smile. "I thought we already were."

Naomi blushed slightly. "I believe you are right." She stood to her feet. "Please let me know what happens with this situation. I would not worry. Gott is watching over you."

Cheryl stood to her feet, her ankle sending a twinge to remind her of her injury. "Naomi, did you remember to ask Levi about the note?"

"Ja," she said, frowning. "He had been looking for his Bible, and as I guessed, he accidentally left it here when he made his delivery. But he knows nothing of the note and could not guess where it came from."

"Maybe someone put it inside the Bible while it was in the shop," Cheryl said. "Guess I can just add it to the other mysterious things going on at the Swiss Miss."

"I am sorry you are distressed," Naomi said. "I will pray for you."

"Thank you. It seems I need it."

There was a knock at the door before it slowly swung open.

"I am sorry to interrupt," Esther said, "but I am supposed to meet Lydia in a few minutes. We are going to the bookstore."

Cheryl tried to hide a smile. Many Amish young people loved to read, especially the so-called bonnet books that centered around their simple community. Although reading fiction wasn't forbidden under the community's *Ordnung*, a set of rules and regulations specifically in place for each local district, many of the older people found it hard to understand why their children weren't content with just reading the Bible. Naomi was very sympathetic with Esther's love of literature, but having been raised on the Bible and a few religious books approved by their church, she had told Cheryl that Esther and Lydia's interests were a little difficult for her to accept.

Naomi frowned at her daughter. "Another book?"

Esther grinned. "Ja, *Maam*. Another book. You should not worry about me so. I am careful in what I read."

Naomi sniffed. "'A mother is a gardener of Gott, tending to the hearts of her children.'"

Cheryl recognized the Amish proverb Naomi quoted. Aunt Mitzi had grown to love the wisdom of these proverbs. In fact, she had several samplers in her house with some of her favorite sayings.

Not missing a beat, Esther shot back, "Ja, and 'good character, like good soup, is usually homemade.'" She smiled at her mother. "You and *Daed* have given me good character. I hope you trust this is true."

Naomi sighed deeply. "You push my patience, Esther. Buy your book. I need to visit with the Yoders about an order. Then I will come by the bookstore to pick you up."

Esther laughed and then came over to give her mother a big hug. "I love you, Maam."

Naomi's lips twitched in a smile. "I love you too. Now off with you. Do not dawdle. You know your daed likes his supper served on time."

After casting a quick grin at Cheryl, Esther left the office. The women heard the bell over the front door ring as she left.

"She's a wonderful girl," Cheryl said softly.

Naomi nodded. "Ja, I know this is true. I trust she will continue to make good choices and follow Gott's ways."

Naomi's words were positive, but Cheryl could see the concern on her face. "I'm sure she will."

"I must be on my way as well," Naomi said. "I will be praying for you and for the woman who is the recipient of so much anger. And I will also pray for the man so full of rage. He must be very unhappy."

Cheryl wasn't surprised at Naomi's response. This was the Amish way. Forgiveness toward everyone. But she did feel some slight conviction since her attitude toward the man in the maze wasn't quite so magnanimous. As she walked Naomi to the door, she asked, "Did you happen to mention my interest in the Bible covers to Levi?"

Naomi stopped and looked at her strangely. "Ja, and he seemed to consider it. I am surprised since he was so against the idea when Mitzi addressed it." She shook her head. "Levi said he will speak to you soon about the possibility." She reached over and touched Cheryl's arm. "You have not yet seen our farm. Would you like to have dinner with us tomorrow night? You could talk to him then."

Cheryl smiled. "I would love it, Naomi. Thank you."

The Amish woman nodded, a look of satisfaction on her face. "Can you be at our house at six o'clock?"

"Yes, I look forward to it."

"*Gut*." With one last smile, Naomi went out to her buggy, got inside, and drove away.

Cheryl worked until five o'clock, closed the store, and headed home. As she walked, she kept looking behind her. Even though she didn't notice anything unusual, she had the strangest feeling she was being watched.

CHAPTER FOUR

After a quick dinner of leftover spaghetti from the night before, Cheryl settled down on the couch to watch some TV, a small fire crackling in the fireplace. Beau jumped up next to her, curled into a ball, and began to purr contentedly. Before flipping on the television, Cheryl turned the day's events over in her mind. Had she overreacted to the man in the corn maze? Did Naomi think she was silly to get so upset? Cheryl's ankle still throbbed, and she realized how absurd she must seem to the gentle Amish woman. Of course, Naomi would never let Cheryl know she found her ridiculous. She was too nice for that. Cheryl sighed deeply. Everything had been going so well. Why did something have to happen to disturb her peaceful new life?

She noticed the mail on the lamp table next to the couch and picked it up. She'd been dumping it on the table ever since Mitzi left, but the pile was getting a little high. Mitzi had told her to put all the mail in a big basket in her bedroom, but Cheryl just hadn't taken the time to do it yet. She grabbed the stack, intending to carry it to her aunt's room, when she noticed a newspaper stuck between the envelopes and circulars. She took it out and left it on the table to read later. Then she headed for the bedroom. As she leaned over to put the mail in the basket, she noticed a yellow envelope lying at the bottom. With a smile, she bent over and picked it up. Down through the years, her aunt had developed a habit of sending her niece letters to encourage her. The envelopes were always yellow. "Yellow is such a happy color," Aunt Mitzi liked to say. "It reminds me of sunshine. When you see my yellow envelope, you'll know I'm sending some sunshine your way."

After putting the mail in the basket, Cheryl carried the letter back into the living room. Once again she plopped down on the couch. Then she opened the envelope and pulled out the letter inside.

My dearest niece,

By the time you read this, I will be living my dream. Our group will be stationed in a very rural area where the people live in huts without electricity or plumbing. They have had very little education and most cannot read, so sharing the love of God with them must be verbal. There are many different languages in Papua New Guinea. Thankfully, we will have a translator who travels with us. He knows several languages, more than enough to get us by. I'm afraid we will end up keeping the poor man very busy.

The people in Papua New Guinea have many spirit gods, so the challenge is to make them understand that Christ is not a god to add to the list—but the One and Only God.

Cheryl shook her head as she read her aunt's words. She had a desire to share Christ too, but the idea of existing without electricity or plumbing appalled her. Obviously Mitzi wasn't worried at all about the kind of living conditions she was facing.

"Thank You, God, for creating people who love going to places like this," Cheryl said softly. "It's certainly not the kind of life for me."

Beau's soft mewing made her smile. "I don't think you'd like it either, boy." She went back to her aunt's letter.

I left you this "sunshine" letter to remind you that I will be praying for you every day, asking God to help you find your way in Sugarcreek. Just like my surroundings will be new to me, I know Sugarcreek will not be what you're used to. Trying new things leads us to discover all the treasures God has already prepared for us, making our journey so exciting! I believe you and I will bloom beautifully in these new gardens where God has planted us. We are where we are for a reason, and if we allow God to work, He will use us to produce great crops of blessings for those He sends into our lives. My calling is no more important than yours, honey. God has created each of us differently, but no one person's work has a higher value than another's.

I encourage you to look forward to each day God has given you. The past is behind you. Don't let it affect your joy. The Amish say it this way: "Regrets of the past and the fear of tomorrow are twin thieves that rob us of the moment." I pray you will give Him your past and trust Him with your future. I know that He has a great plan for your life, and I am so thrilled to be a part of it!

I will be waiting to hear all the good news from Sugarcreek—just remember what I told you about our mail. It will likely take a while for our letters to reach each other. If you want to write, you can send your letters to the mission address I left for you. The good folks there will get them to me as soon as they can.

Know that you are deeply and truly loved, my dear, sweet girl.

Aunt Mitzi

Cheryl slid the letter back into its envelope. How did her aunt always manage to convey just the right message at the exact right moment? As long as Cheryl could remember, it had been this way. Mitzi was still doing it, even from thousands of miles away. Cheryl blinked back the tears that filled her eyes. She wouldn't let today's strange circumstances ruin her belief that she was exactly where God wanted her to be. If He'd sent her here, He would also take care of her.

"All we can do is take each day at a time," she said to Beau.

He meowed again and stretched out his paw, placing it on her leg.

"You silly old cat. I know you're lonely when I'm at work. Maybe I'll take you to the shop tomorrow, but if I do, you'll have to behave."

Beau rolled over on his back and stared at her upside down, giving her a comical smile that made her laugh. "You really are a goofy feline. We'll give it a try, but you have to stay off the counters and away from the food."

For the most part, Beau was a very well-behaved cat, so Cheryl wasn't too worried about taking him to the Swiss Miss. She could keep his food and his litter box in the bathroom off the office. He would certainly be happier with people around. Beau was a very sociable cat.

Once again, Cheryl started to turn on the TV, but then she remembered the newspaper. She leaned over and picked it up. *The Budget*. It was a newspaper produced in Sugarcreek that was mailed out all across the country. Aunt Mitzi had mentioned it. Instead of watching television, Cheryl settled down to read the interesting Mennonite/Amish-based publication. She read until she grew sleepy, then she and Beau headed to bed.

The next morning, with Beau inside his carrying crate, Cheryl drove her car the few blocks to work. She also had an extra litter box, food, and bowls, and an assortment of cat toys to keep him amused, although she was pretty sure her customers would provide all the entertainment the friendly Siamese would need.

She pulled up to the Swiss Miss and began unloading Beau and his possessions. Once inside, he began sniffing out his new digs, exploring every nook and cranny with delight.

Cheryl kept an eye on him as customers came in the door. He seemed to size each one up and only approached if they called to him or smiled when they noticed his presence. But anyone who didn't seem interested received the same response in return. He repaid their indifference by turning his back, his tail held high, and walking away, which seemed to be a feline expression of contempt. Cheryl had to stifle a giggle more than once.

Around nine o'clock Rueben Vogel came in and went straight to the checkers table. A few minutes later, Ben entered. He tipped his head toward Cheryl, which was his way of saying hello. She returned his nod with a smile and watched as he took his usual seat across from his brother. Without a word or any kind of acknowledgment, Rueben made the first move. Cheryl had noticed that whoever arrived first started the game. It seemed to be an unspoken rule.

Cheryl marveled at the similarities between the two men. Though dressed differently, the men were almost identical twins. Rueben wore the usual Amish garb—dark pants, white shirt with suspenders, and a large straw hat, which he removed when he sat down. Ben wore casual slacks and a short-sleeved blue shirt. Rueben's beard was big and full while Ben's was short and neat, but besides that, there were very few differences in their appearance. Both men were tall, thin, and wiry, but to assume their slender frames meant they were weak would be a mistake. Years of hard work had made them strong, and working out in the sun had browned and toughened their skin. The shapes of their faces were almost identical, long and narrow with wide mouths planted beneath rather large, bulbous noses. But the features that stood out most were their startling blue eyes. Light blue, the color of a cloudless sky, they didn't seem to fit their weathered features.

A young woman had just come up to the counter and asked about the price of a quilted apron when Cheryl noticed something that made her gasp. Slowly but surely, Beau was headed toward the Vogel brothers. Afraid he would annoy them and interrupt their game, Cheryl stepped around the corner, ready to run out and grab him, but she wasn't fast enough. The cat sat down next to Rueben's chair and stared up at him. For just a moment, both brothers looked down at Beau. Then Rueben reached down and began to rub his head. Beau's loud purring made it clear he'd just made a new friend. Relieved, Cheryl went back to her customer and finished answering her question. The woman decided to buy the apron so Cheryl quickly checked her out. When she swung her attention back to the brothers, they were both concentrating on their game with Beau curled up under the table between them. Cheryl had never actually talked to either one of the brothers, afraid she'd do or say something stupid and ruin their fragile relationship. Leave it to an animal to teach its human counterparts how to bridge a delicate emotional gap.

"Miss Cooper?"

Cheryl jumped at the sound of a male voice. As she turned her head, she found herself staring into Levi Miller's dark blue eyes. She realized that, although the Vogel brothers' eyes reminded her of a morning sky, Levi's eyes were the deep blue of a sky at night, framed by long lashes and a rugged but handsome face. Cheryl found herself reacting in a way that wasn't appropriate toward an Amish man. Although he'd been by the store several times, for some reason she'd never noticed how good-looking he actually was. Gulping, she smiled as she tried to rein in feelings she didn't understand or welcome.

"Levi," she finally said. "I...I'm sorry. I was distracted, and I didn't see you come in."

He smiled. "I can see that. Perhaps this is not a good time to talk to you?"

She shook her head. Except for the Vogel brothers, no one else was in the store. Taking a deep breath, she tried to calm her nerves. What was wrong with her? She was being silly.

"It's fine. And please call me Cheryl."

"Maam says you are interested in the Bible covers I make?"

Cheryl nodded. "They're beautiful. I'd love to offer them in the store. Your mother said you'd already turned my aunt down, but I had to ask again. I've never seen covers as wonderfully crafted as yours. I know people would buy them."

Levi was quiet for a moment. "They take a long time to create. So far I have only made them as gifts for friends and family." He rubbed his bare chin with one hand while he considered her offer. Since he was single, he didn't have the beard worn by Amish men who were married. "How many would you need and how often?" he asked finally.

"That's up to you, Levi," Cheryl said. "There's no pressure. Just bring by whatever you have, and I'll put them on the shelf. When one sells, I'll keep thirty percent, and you'll get seventy percent."

He nodded. "That sounds fair. But how much do you think I should charge for each cover?"

"Another shop in town offers them for sixty-five dollars, and those covers aren't nearly as nice as yours. I would say at least seventy-five for the simpler ones and one hundred dollars for more intricate covers."

Levi's eyebrows shot up. "That much? I must say I am surprised." He was quiet for a moment. "All right," he said finally. "I will do it. The money would certainly help my family." His eyes met Cheryl's. "But I cannot allow this to take time away from helping Daed around the farm. I will work on these at night."

"Do you have any already made?" Cheryl asked.

He nodded. "I have four that are completed. I will bring them to you later today."

Cheryl smiled. "Actually, I can pick them up tonight. Your mother invited me to supper."

Levi returned her smile. "I am happy you will be sharing a meal with us. Maam is a wonderful cook."

Cheryl nodded. "Everything she brings to the store sells very well."

Levi chuckled. "Wait until you taste her fried chicken. Maam would scold me for bragging if she heard me say this, but it is not so much brag as fact—her cookin' is the best in the county."

"Now you're making me hungry."

Cheryl was immediately drawn to his hearty, rich laugh. It seemed to come from somewhere deep inside him.

"Cheryl, before I go, may I ask about a note you found in my Bible? Maam told me about it. I do not know where it came from. The entire situation is very confusing."

"Yes, it is," she told him. "I have no idea who put it there. To be honest, quite a few odd things have happened lately. The note is just the latest."

Levi pushed back a lock of longish blond hair. "I will ask around. If I find out how the message got into my Bible, I will let you know. No one at home would do such a thing. The only other time my Bible might have been unattended was during a church meeting, but I cannot imagine that anyone there would write a note like this."

"We may never know where it came from. I'm sure everything is fine. Probably just a simple mistake."

Levi frowned. "Perhaps, but I do not like the spirit behind it. It does not seem . . . right."

"I understand what you mean."

"Well, I must be going, but I will see you tonight, Cheryl. I look forward to your company."

Cheryl nodded and said good-bye. She watched him as he left. "I must be getting desperate," she said quietly to herself. Being attracted to an Amish man was ridiculous, and she had no intention of ruining her relationship with Naomi. "That's enough of that," she said in a low voice as she bent down to get a new pen for her order pad.

"Enough of what?" a voice said from behind her.

Cheryl jumped, stood up straight, and whirled around to find Lydia Troyer standing next to her. It was the second time in a row someone had startled her. Obviously, her nerves were on edge. "You scared me," she said to Lydia, with a chuckle.

"I am sorry," the young girl said, "but I thought you wanted me to come in today and do inventory?"

"Yes. Yes, I do. I'd forgotten I'd already asked you. Several items have popped up on my shelves that I don't recognize. I need to know if my lists are wrong."

Cheryl surveyed the Amish girl. Her usual modest dress had been replaced with jeans, flats, and a dark blue blouse. Her prayer covering was gone, and instead, her long black hair was held back by clips on each side. She was also wearing a little mascara and a light application of pink lipstick. Rumspringa had struck again.

"I know I look different," Lydia said hesitantly. "Perhaps you only want people who work for you to wear typical Amish clothing?"

"No, Lydia," Cheryl said gently. "As long as your clothes are appropriate for work, I don't care what you wear. That's your decision. You do need to put on an apron though."

The girl nodded. "Maam and Daed are not happy with the clothes my *Englisch* friend gave me, but they do not say anything. I have the right to choose what I want."

"Yes, you do. I think you look very pretty." Cheryl felt a little torn inside by Lydia's choices. Although Cheryl didn't believe God's love and acceptance had anything to do with clothing choices, her friendship with Naomi had given her a small glance inside the Amish world. She realized that Naomi was concerned about worldly influences that might corrupt Esther. It was clear that the loss of Sarah haunted her, and that she was afraid of losing Esther as well.

"Thank you," Lydia said, her face lighting up. "I think so too, but no one says so. I keep telling Esther to give the Englisch ways a try, but she is too afraid."

Cheryl frowned at the girl. "She needs to make her own decisions, Lydia. Just like you. Isn't that what rumspringa is all about?"

"Sure. But sometimes friends need help to see the truth."

Her rather petulant tone made it clear Lydia wasn't really open to anyone's opinion but her own.

"Why don't you get the inventory book in my office and get started," Cheryl suggested, cutting the conversation short.

"Okay." Lydia grabbed a clean apron from under the counter, and then flounced off, coming back about a minute later, wearing her apron and holding the book and a pencil. She'd taken inventory before for Mitzi, so she didn't ask Cheryl any questions, just set about her work while Cheryl helped a group of women who'd come into the shop together. Cheryl had just rung up their purchases when Lydia came back to the counter with a puzzled look on her face. Cheryl quickly completed the transactions and said goodbye to her customers. Then she turned her attention to Lydia.

"I found one of those...strange things on a shelf," Lydia said. She handed Cheryl a beautifully painted china plate. Red, blue, and yellow flowers in a purple vase. The colors and shapes were eye-catching.

"Okay," Cheryl said with a sigh.

"This was next to it." She handed Cheryl a white envelope with her name written on the outside.

Cheryl took it willingly. Was the creator of all the homemade items finally coming out of hiding? Feeling a rush of anticipation, Cheryl tore open the envelope and pulled out a piece of paper. But instead of excitement, her emotions turned an entirely different direction as she read:

Keep quiet or you'll be very, very sorry.

CHAPTER FIVE

A re you all right, Cheryl?"

Cheryl realized her reaction to the letter concerned the young Amish girl. Shaking off the shock of reading an obvious threat aimed at her, Cheryl smiled at Lydia. "I'm fine. Sorry. Just a personal note from a customer. Nothing important." She didn't want to be rude or dismissive of Lydia, but she needed time to think. She urged Lydia to get back to her inventory work, trying not to look as alarmed as she felt. Then she slid the note into her apron pocket. Could the person leaving the gifts have written this? Cheryl couldn't believe it. The beautiful craft items and the crude note just didn't go together. As she was wondering what to do next, Naomi came in the front door. Cheryl hesitated a moment. Should she keep silent? What if she put her new friend in harm's way?

"I have brought you more raspberry jam. I noticed you were getting low..." Naomi stopped and stared at Cheryl.

Before she could say another word, Cheryl took the basket of jam from Naomi. She shook her head slightly, hoping her friend would take the hint that she needed her to be quiet in front of Lydia.

"Please watch the register, Lydia. I need to talk to Naomi about her order."

Lydia nodded and began walking toward the front counter while Cheryl quickly scanned the store. Besides the Vogel brothers and Beau, there was a man and two women looking over her stock. She didn't know any of them and couldn't take a chance they might think she was going to say something she shouldn't to Naomi.

"I have a problem with your last delivery," Cheryl said rather loudly. "We need to talk about it."

She went to the office door and swung it open, motioning for Naomi to go inside. Once both women were safely within the small room, Cheryl closed the door and locked it.

"Is...is everything all right?" Naomi asked. "Did I bring you something you did not like?"

Cheryl waved her hand dismissively. "No, of course not. I had to get you in here so I could show you something. I'm sorry about what I said, but I was trying to be careful. I didn't want anyone to think I was telling you...what I'm about to tell you."

Naomi frowned at her. "Has something else happened?"

Cheryl took a seat in one of the chairs in front of her desk and pulled the other chair closer. After putting the basket of jams on her desk, Naomi sat down next to her.

"Lydia found this on a shelf—next to a painted plate that isn't part of my inventory. At first I thought the items were related, but after thinking about it, I'm not so sure about that. Why would someone give me gifts and threaten me at the same time?"

Naomi took the note from Cheryl and read it. Her face paled. "Oh, Cheryl, this is not right. I believe it is time to talk to Chief Twitchell at the police department."

Cheryl sighed. "I don't know. The note says I should keep quiet. What if the person who wrote this finds out I contacted the authorities?" She looked into Naomi's eyes. "What should I do?"

Naomi stared back at Cheryl for several seconds. "I...I do not know," she said finally. "Why don't you bring this note, along with the other one, to my house tonight? I would like to see what Seth and Levi have to say. I have found their advice to be very wise."

"But that means telling more people, Naomi," Cheryl said, unable to keep a note of anxiety from creeping into her voice. "Exactly what the note warns me not to do."

"You are coming to our home for a meal, Cheryl," Naomi said firmly. "No one will think that is odd. And besides, I do not believe anyone who would write a note like this would be very concerned about an Amish family, ain't so?"

Even though the strange message had shaken her, Cheryl had to chuckle. "You're probably right."

Although she wanted to believe she was equal to handling the situation alone, Cheryl remembered a scripture from Proverbs, chapter twenty, verse eighteen: "Plans are established by seeking advice; so if you wage war, obtain guidance." In Cheryl's mind, she was in a war. Someone wanted to disrupt the peace she'd found in Sugarcreek, and she had no intention of letting that happen.

"All right," she said finally. "If you don't think Seth and Levi will mind, I would really like to hear what they have to say."

"I am sure they will be more than happy to share their thoughts. After all, they are men, ja?"

Naomi's attempt at humor made Cheryl laugh. "You're right about that. They are men."

The two women smiled at each other as if sharing a secret. Cheryl already felt better. "I can't tell you how much I appreciate you and your family. I...I was afraid of being alone after my aunt left."

"You are never alone, Cheryl," Naomi said. "Gott is always with you. It is He who gives us friends. 'Love always finds a home in the heart of a friend.'"

Cheryl recognized that particular Amish proverb. Mitzi had embroidered the saying, and it was framed and hanging on the wall in her living room.

"Thank you," Cheryl said. She tried to blink away the quick tears that filled her eyes.

Naomi reached over and patted her arm. "I am blessed by you as well, my friend. We will face this...this trial together. Gott will see us through."

Cheryl nodded, unable to trust herself to speak.

Naomi stood to her feet. "I must go, but we will see you tonight at six o'clock. Do you know how to find our farm?"

"I think so. At the end of Main Street there's a sign that points the way to the Miller Maze and Petting Zoo. I assume if I follow the sign, I will come across your house?"

Naomi smiled. "Yes. You will see our home not long after passing the maze and the zoo. We will be watching for you."

Cheryl stood up and gave her friend a hug. "I'll see you tonight. And thank you again."

Naomi patted Cheryl on the back before letting her go. Then she pointed at the basket of jam on the desk. "I think you will find the jam to be especially good."

Cheryl dabbed at her cheeks with her fingers. "I'm sure of that. Sorry about what I said to get you in here."

"A truly humble person is not easily offended."

Cheryl smiled. "Another proverb?"

Naomi nodded. "One that is still hard for me to follow sometimes, I am afraid."

She glanced toward the closed office door, and Cheryl wondered if she was thinking about Lydia.

"An attribute that's difficult for all of us, I'm afraid," Cheryl said. She opened the door to her office, and she and Naomi walked out. Lydia stood behind the counter.

"Is everything all right?" she asked in a concerned voice.

Naomi took in the girl's modern clothes as if she hadn't noticed them the first time. A look of disapproval colored her features, but she didn't say anything.

"Everything is fine, Lydia," Cheryl said quickly. "Just a misunderstanding."

Lydia looked relieved. "Good."

"I must be on my way," Naomi said to Cheryl, pointedly ignoring Lydia. "I look forward to your visit tonight."

Naomi quickly went out the front door and got into her buggy.

"She doesn't like me anymore," Lydia said softly.

Cheryl could hear the hurt in her voice. "She likes you, Lydia. She's just concerned about Esther. Surely you can understand that."

"Not really."

Cheryl frowned at the girl. "Don't your parents worry about you?"

Lydia shrugged. "They do not want me to leave the church, but they also want me to be sure about my commitment to Gott." Lydia shook her head. "I don't want to follow Him just because my parents choose to."

Cheryl could understand the girl's argument, but in Lydia's case, she wondered if she might just be repeating something her parents had told her, while Esther seemed to be sincerely searching her heart. Cheryl got the feeling Lydia enjoyed the attention her choices were bringing her. As if confirming her suspicions, a family came in the front door with a teenage son in tow. His eyes widened when he saw Lydia. She tossed her hair and smiled at him rather coquettishly.

"Let's get that inventory finished," Cheryl said. Her words came out harsher than she intended. She picked up the inventory book and Lydia's pencil.

The girl took the items, but her smile was replaced with a rather sulky expression. Cheryl found herself feeling a little irritated, but why should she be? She wasn't Amish. What the girl did wasn't Cheryl's business—as long as it didn't interfere with her work.

The morning was fairly busy, and around noon Esther came in. Cheryl went to her office to eat. She'd brought lunch for herself and for Beau. He seemed a little lost after the Vogel brothers left and had spent the rest of the morning schmoozing up to other customers, especially the children. But when he smelled his favorite meal being served in the back room, he made a beeline for the office.

"You're a pill," she told him as he gulped down his tuna cat food. The aroma overshadowed the peanut butter and jelly sandwich Cheryl was trying to eat. "Tuna and peanut butter. Yuck," she said to Beau, who ignored her completely.

After lunch, Cheryl worked on the books until it was time for Esther to leave. When Cheryl went back into the shop, she was surprised to find Rachel Swartzentruber and another woman looking over the cooler of cheese and fruit. According to Mitzi, the Swartzentrubers were one of Sugarcreek's most respected families. Cheryl was eager to get to know Rachel. Aunt Mitzi said Rachel had been raised English before she joined the Amish church and married her husband. Cheryl met Rachel when she first came to Sugarcreek but hadn't run into her even once after that. Cheryl assumed it was due to the fact that Rachel was expecting her first baby and, by the looks of her now, he or she would make an appearance rather soon. Rachel likely wanted to keep close to home lest she go into labor.

"She used to come into the shop at least a couple of times a week," Aunt Mitzi had told Cheryl. "And then suddenly it seemed as if she didn't want to leave her house. I went by to check on her recently to make sure she wasn't having problems with her pregnancy." Mitzi had shrugged. "She said she was fine, just that her cousin, Martha, was staying with them for a while."

"Hello, Rachel," Cheryl said, smiling at the Amish woman. "It's good to see you."

Rachel nodded briefly. "Hello, Cheryl." She rested her hand on her large baby bump. "Have you met my cousin, Martha?"

"No, I haven't." Cheryl held her hand out to the woman who stood next to Rachel. Martha shook her hand lightly but only looked up briefly. Cheryl got a quick glimpse of a pale woman with wide green eyes and reddish brown hair covered by a large black bonnet. Cheryl had seen bonnets before, sometimes worn instead of a lighter prayer covering or Amish *kapp*, but this one extended so far forward that it hid most of Martha's face. "I'm glad to meet you, Martha," Cheryl said. Although the woman nodded, she didn't say anything.

"I wonder if you have butter cheese?" Rachel asked. "I've been craving it...or maybe it's these two who have the cravings." She patted her midsection.

"Oh, you are having twins? How wonderful!" Cheryl exclaimed. "Do you know if they are boys or girls or one of each?"

Rachel smiled. "We will wait until they arrive to see how the Lord has blessed us."

"Well, I am delighted for you. They will bring twice the joy, I am sure," Cheryl said. "Now, how much of this cheese will satisfy your cravings?" She smiled.

Rachel thought for a moment. "A pound should do it."

While Cheryl talked to Rachel, she noticed Martha kept her gaze focused on her feet. She seemed unusually shy.

Cheryl went to the cooler and picked up a one-pound package of butter cheese, a cheese she'd never heard of until coming to

Ohio. It was now one of her favorites. Mild and smooth, it went with almost everything.

Cheryl met the women at the counter and was getting ready to ring up their purchase when Lydia and Esther came up next to her.

"Is it all right for us to leave now?" Lydia asked. "It's a few minutes past three."

Cheryl nodded. "Thank you, girls." She smiled at Esther. "I'll see you tonight at your house."

"I am so glad you are coming for supper," Esther said slowly.

Cheryl noticed an uneasy look on her face. "Is everything all right?"

Esther reached into her apron pocket and pulled out a piece of paper, handing it to Cheryl. "I found this on the floor. Is it yours?"

Not recognizing it at first, Cheryl flipped it open. It was the note warning her to keep quiet. It must have fallen out of her pocket. Although she closed it as quickly as possible, she wasn't quite fast enough. She looked up to see Martha staring at the words on the paper, her eyes wide. Before Cheryl could explain, Martha's face went white and she collapsed to the floor.

CHAPTER SIX

"A re you sure you're feeling better?" Cheryl wiped Martha's face once more with the cool cloth she'd prepared. She and Rachel were in the office while Lydia and Esther watched the shop.

"Yes, I'm fine," Martha said, gently pushing Cheryl's hand away. "I...I'm sorry. I didn't mean to make a scene. I haven't been feeling well..."

Cheryl walked to the bathroom and put the damp washcloth in the sink. She wondered what to say to the distressed woman. She was clearly upset. It was obvious to her that Martha and Rachel were trying to hide something.

"We need to go home," Rachel said when Cheryl came back into the office. "Martha needs to rest." She gave Cheryl a tremulous smile. "I would appreciate it if you would not tell anyone about Martha's...condition. We would not want anyone to worry unnecessarily."

Cheryl nodded. "I won't say anything, but I can't speak for Esther and Lydia."

Rachel frowned, and she reached out to grab Cheryl's arm. "Perhaps you could ask them to keep this situation quiet?"

"I...I can do that, but I'd really appreciate it if you would tell me the truth."

"I have no idea what you mean," Rachel said, the color draining from her face.

For a moment, Cheryl wondered if she might faint, just as Martha had. A panicky thought crossed Cheryl's mind that she might have thrown Rachel into early labor. "Please sit down," she said to the Amish woman. Cheryl helped her into the chair next to her cousin. Then Cheryl walked around the desk and sat down in the desk chair. Rachel appeared to have regained her composure.

"Look," she said gently, "I don't usually get into other people's business, but I'm afraid I have to this time." She gazed directly at Martha. "You reacted to a note left for me. I want to know why." She held up her hand. "And you might as well tell me who you really are. Unless you recently became Amish, you're hiding your true identity."

"What do you mean?" Martha asked.

Cheryl could see the fear in the woman's eyes, and it touched her heart. "Your earlobes are pierced, and although I can't see much of your hair, I can tell it was streaked a few months ago. And your nails. Those nails have been manicured professionally." She swung her gaze to Rachel. "You can trust me, Rachel. I don't plan to tell anyone what you share with me. But whatever's going on seems to have involved me as well. I think you need to let me in on it, don't you?"

Rachel's eyes locked onto Martha's, and they stared at each other for several seconds before Martha sighed and leaned back into her chair.

"I'll explain everything," she said. "But if you tell anyone else, I'll have to leave town. And that could be very dangerous."

Cheryl nodded. "All right."

"Do you know Janie Henderson?"

"Yes. She owns Sunshine Stables. She comes in here sometimes. A very nice lady."

Martha nodded. "Yes, she is. Janie and I went to high school together. My real name is Abby. Abby Harper. A few months ago, I ran into Janie at our twenty-year reunion in Canton. Although I tried to hide it, Janie could tell that..." She stopped talking and seemed to look to Rachel for help.

"Let's just say that for her own safety, Abby needed to leave her husband," Rachel said softly, "before her situation got any worse."

Abby nodded. "Sometimes makeup can't hide everything." Her voice was so soft, Cheryl almost couldn't hear her.

"I'm so sorry," Cheryl said. "So why are you here? In Sugarcreek?"

Abby took a deep breath as if trying to draw on some kind of inner strength. "Janie told me I couldn't go back. Couldn't allow Jerry to hurt me again."

As Abby wrapped her arms around herself, Cheryl noticed she was trembling. She fought back tears of compassion.

"I did go home, but only long enough to pack."

"She was afraid he would try to force her to remain under his control," Rachel interjected. "She had no choice but to disappear."

Abby nodded. "Yes. In the past, threats to leave caused nothing but fights. H...he told me if I ever tried to leave him, he would kill me. I believe him."

"Did you call the police?" Cheryl asked.

Abby sighed. "No. We live in a small town in Nebraska. Jerry went to school with the police chief. They're buddies. I couldn't trust him to take my side."

"He might have."

Abby nodded. "Yes, maybe. But I was too afraid to take a chance."

"So you came here? To Sugarcreek?"

She nodded. "Yes. I took a tour bus here. Under an assumed name. Once I was in town, Janie introduced me to Rachel. She agreed to let me stay with them. Hide out as an Amish woman. The idea was to disappear for a while and then contact a women's shelter when I felt it was safe."

"Why haven't you done that?"

"Because a friend who knows us told me that Jerry is on the warpath. He's determined to find me, and my friend said he was staking out women's shelters in this area. I realize they don't release information about their clients, but... well, Jerry is very persistent. I was afraid he'd figure out where I was hiding." The panic in her face was obvious. "He's already been to Canton, asking old classmates who I talked to at the reunion. I've been worried he might come here—because of Janie. He knows we were friends."

Cheryl frowned. "But what does that have to do with the note?" As soon as she asked the question, she was sure of the answer. "It's his handwriting."

Abby nodded. "Yes, I'd know it anywhere."

Although Cheryl didn't want to add to the woman's fear, she quickly told her about her experience in the corn maze. "I have to wonder if that was your husband."

Abby put her hand on her chest. "Oh no. I should leave here. I don't want to involve other people in my problems."

Rachel reached over and grabbed Abby's arm. "You do not know it was him, Abby." She pointed at the note still lying on Cheryl's desk. "And maybe this is not his writing. Perhaps it is just similar."

"I just remembered," Cheryl said. "He mentioned a name. I'd forgotten about it until just now. The rest of the message disturbed me so much, it dropped out of my head."

"What was the name?" Abby asked.

"Arch. He was talking to someone named Arch."

"That's Archie. His brother." She turned to Rachel. "It was definitely him."

"Then we must get you home immediately." Rachel looked over at Cheryl. "Did you see this man? Do you know what he looks like?"

Cheryl shook her head. "He was hidden by the maze. If he walked right up to me, I wouldn't recognize him. I'm sorry."

"That's all right," Abby said. "I've got to get where it's safe— and think about what to do next."

"Look," Cheryl said. "I heard him threaten you. And this note proves he's also threatened me. I believe the police here will help you."

Abby shook her head. "You overheard a man on a phone, Cheryl. You can't prove it was him. Nor can you prove who wrote this note. He hasn't done anything the police can arrest him for. I went through all of this before we moved to Nebraska. I was told he'd have to actually hurt me again for the police to step in."

"What about taking out a restraining order?" Cheryl asked.

"I tried all that too. He doesn't care about them. And he told me if I ever filed one again, he'd make me pay." She stood unsteadily to her feet. "I've got to leave Sugarcreek. I'm putting you all in danger."

"Abby, please give me some time," Cheryl said. "Let's me see if I can think of something. Maybe we can at least convince him you're not in town so he'll take off. That would give you some time to figure out what to do."

Rachel nodded and reached for Abby's arm. "I agree, Abby. It is better to stand your ground and confront the situation here. With people who love you, ja?"

The tears in Abby's eyes spilled over. "I can't believe you care about me so much. You don't owe me anything. I must seem so foolish to you. To allow myself to get involved with a man like this."

"'The only time to look down on your neighbor is when you're bending over to help,'" Rachel said.

Abby put her hand over her mouth to stifle a sob. Finally, she nodded. "Okay, I'll stay. For now."

"Ach, Gott will deliver you," Rachel said. "You must have faith."

"I'm trying." Abby's eyes filled with tears. "It's very difficult."

Cheryl picked up the note and put it back in her pocket. "This message was for me because I overheard him in the corn maze.

That doesn't mean Jerry knows you're here, Abby. Since he obviously hasn't found you, and he could already be gone. Maybe he's on his way to search for you somewhere else."

"That would be wonderful," Abby said.

The hope on her face made Cheryl's determination to help the woman even stronger. "You two go home. And don't go out, Abby. For any reason."

"All right," she replied softly. "But if I ever believe my presence here will put you in the line of fire, I'll leave. And nothing you can say will stop me."

"All right. I understand." As Cheryl stood up and walked to the office door, she thought of something. "Do you have a picture of Jerry?"

"I've never carried one in my wallet, and I didn't take any pictures of us when I left. For obvious reasons."

"It would help if I knew what he looked like."

Abby sighed. "He's medium height, brown hair. Older than me. Mid-fifties. There's nothing that stands out about him." She paused for a moment. Then she snapped her fingers. "Except for his tattoo. He has a tattoo of a tiger on his upper right arm."

"It's October," Cheryl said. "Not too many men are wearing sleeveless shirts."

"I wish I could give you more information, something that would help you," Abby said. "But Jerry is one of those people who doesn't stand out in a crowd. And to be honest, he may even be wearing a disguise."

"Why do you say that, Abby?" Rachel asked.

"Because he's done it before. Once when I took out a restraining order, he showed up in my neighborhood dressed like someone from the telephone company. He even wore a wig and a mustache."

Cheryl grunted. "Finding him is going to be difficult if I don't even know what he looks like." She thought for a moment. "What about social media? Does he have a Facebook page?"

"He doesn't like Facebook—or anything like that, and I wasn't allowed to have a Facebook page. I think it's because he was afraid my family might find out what was going on at home. My parents are living in Colorado now. We moved from Canton after I graduated from high school. Then after I married Jerry, his boss offered him a position in Nebraska where he grew up. Even though I didn't want to move, he accepted the job anyway. As far as my parents know, everything is fine in my marriage."

"Why didn't you go home to Colorado when you left Jerry?" Cheryl asked. "I'm sure your parents would want to help you."

"Because I don't want my family involved in this." Tears ran down Abby's face. "My father didn't want me to marry Jerry, but I didn't listen. I've been too ashamed to tell them what's been going on."

"But I'm sure your parents love you," Cheryl said softly. "Shouldn't you give them a chance instead of hanging on to some false sense of pride?"

Abby shook her head with vigor. "It's not just that. I'm afraid Jerry will hurt them. I've got to find another way. If I can just get him out of my life, I'll gladly go home. It's true that at one time admitting my folks were right was something I was too proud to do. But I don't feel that way anymore. Now it's the least of my concerns."

"Abby, I truly believe you need to contact the local police," Cheryl said. "You need some professional advice and protection."

Abby shook her head. "I think the best thing to do is to keep quiet as long as possible. Until we're sure he's gone. The police here might want to help me, but unless Jerry does something... wrong, there's nothing they can do." Her face was full of fear. "He won't give up, Cheryl. If he finds me, even the police won't be able to stop him. Please. I need time to hide. To think. A chance to make a clean break from him."

"All right." Although Cheryl wasn't certain Abby was making the best decision, she didn't feel it was her place to argue with her. "I'll do everything I can to find out if Jerry is in Sugarcreek. In the meantime, don't go out, whatever you do. If I could tell you're not Amish, other people will notice it too."

"They already have," Rachel said. "I intercepted a note during a church supper last week that said someone in Sugarcreek wasn't who they seemed to be. I'm sure it was directed at Abby."

"I pressured Rachel to let me go to a church meeting," Abby said. "Obviously, it was a mistake."

Cheryl raised an eyebrow. "What did you do with that note, Rachel?"

"I thought I put it inside my Bible, but when I looked later I couldn't find it."

Cheryl smiled. "Let me guess, Levi Miller made your Bible cover."

Rachel's eyes widened. "How do you know this?"

"Because you accidentally put the note in Levi's Bible. He left it here after bringing me a delivery, and the note dropped out."

"Ach," Rachel said. "Well at least I know what happened to it. But it just goes to show that others in our community are suspicious of Abby."

"I'm so sorry to cause all this trouble," Abby said, her voice catching. "Marrying Jerry was my fault. Now innocent people are paying for my mistake."

"A mistake is just a mistake, Abby," Cheryl said. "Trusting the wrong person has happened to most of us." She thought of Lance. Her experience with pain gave her added empathy for Abby. "You need to get going. First let me make sure everything's okay before you go outside." Cheryl opened the door and walked out into the shop. There were two women and a child looking at merchandise. She walked to the front door and looked out. A few people stood across the street, but there were no single men.

She hurried back to her office and told Abby and Rachel to leave quickly. She watched them as they climbed into Rachel's buggy and rode off down Main Street. Abby kept her head down. No one could have seen her face even if they'd wanted to. When Cheryl came inside, she found Esther ringing up a purchase. After the women and the child left together, Cheryl hurried over to where Esther and Lydia stood looking at her strangely.

"You're not to tell anyone about Rachel and her cousin coming to the store today, do you understand? Especially about her cousin's... fainting spell."

The girls nodded, their eyes round with curiosity.

"I mean it." She directed her words to both of them, but she was more concerned about Lydia than she was Esther. "You can go."

Lydia headed for the door, but Esther stayed behind. "Are you all right?" she asked Cheryl. "Can I do anything to help?"

Cheryl shook her head. "Thank you, but no. The only thing you can do to help is to do what I asked. Not a word about Rachel and Martha."

"I will not mention it," she replied. "But I know something is wrong. Martha is not who she seems to be."

The words from the note echoed in Esther's observation, making it even more important that Abby stay off the streets.

"Please, Esther. Don't say that to anyone else. I'll tell you more tonight when I come to your house, but it's very important you not talk about Martha to anyone else."

"I will not," Esther said, frowning. "I trust that you know what you are doing."

"I hope so." Cheryl gave the girl a quick hug.

She watched the girls leave, then she put the Closed sign in the window. She wanted to go home and change before heading to the Millers' farm. After rounding up Beau, she took him to her car and got inside. As she glanced around the streets of Sugarcreek, she realized the small town didn't feel quite as charming as it had before.

Once she got home, she grabbed Beau and hurried inside, quickly closing the door behind her. She doubted seriously that

Jerry Harper was stalking her, but she couldn't shake the feeling that she should be careful. She let Beau out of his carrier and then went into the kitchen. She added some food and water to his bowls and put them back on the floor next to the refrigerator. When she turned around, she found him sitting in the doorway, watching her.

"Don't you start staring at me," she chided him. "You'll make me nervous."

He meowed and began licking his paw. His way of telling her he wasn't taking her warning seriously. Of course, he seemed to take much of what she said with a grain of salt anyway.

"I wish I could be as relaxed as you are," she said as she walked past him and into the bedroom.

She slid off her clothes and looked for something appropriate to wear to the Millers'. Although she was more comfortable in slacks, she decided to wear her dark blue corduroy jumper with a hem that fell below her knees. To go with it, she selected a long-sleeved white blouse. The blouse had small embroidered blue and red flowers on the collar and added a soft, feminine touch to the overall look. Once she was dressed, she looked at herself in the mirror with a critical eye. She looked nice, but more importantly, the outfit was modest enough to make her feel somewhat relaxed about spending time in the home of an Amish family. She chose some tan shoes with small heels and then checked her hair in the mirror. After a quick brushing, she gave up. It was probably as good as it was going to get. Cheryl sighed and put her hairbrush back on her dresser.

"Please, God," she said quietly, "keep me from doing anything embarrassing." As soon as the words left her mouth, Naomi's kind face floated into her mind, and Cheryl smiled. Naomi was the embodiment of graciousness. There was no reason to feel nervous. Actually, Cheryl was looking forward to this evening.

She had just turned to pick up her coat and purse when something passed across her front bedroom window. She gasped and dropped her things back on the bed. Was someone out there? Had Jerry Harper found her? She crept quietly out of the bedroom and into the living room. Thankfully, the drapes were pulled shut so no one could see inside. She stood in the same spot for several seconds, wondering if it had been her imagination. Beau came sauntering into the room, but then he stopped, his ears perked, as if he'd heard something too.

As Cheryl was trying to figure out what to do, she found herself staring at the front door. Had she locked it when she came in? Sometimes she forgot. Another noise from outside paralyzed her, and she couldn't take her eyes off the doorknob. Finally forcing herself to move, she crept closer to the door until she could clearly see it was locked. Breathing a sigh of relief, she walked slowly over to the drapes and moved them aside just enough until she could see the front porch. Sure enough, a figure stood by the door, hunched over like he was trying to see into the house. She quickly closed the drapes and grabbed her cell phone. Should she call the police? What if it wasn't Jerry Harper? She didn't want to look like a fool.

As she thought about her options, she realized she couldn't open the front door. She was certain she hadn't locked the screen door. She never did that until right before she went to bed at night. If she opened the door now, whoever was out there could push his way inside. Not knowing what else to do, she hurried to the back door and opened it slowly. After looking around and seeing no one, she closed it quietly behind her and made her way around the side of the house, praying with each step she took. She punched 911 into her phone but didn't press *Send*. At least she was prepared in case she needed help.

When she finally reached the front of the house, she peered around the corner. The man was still there. She watched as he moved away from the front door and tried to look through the window. Then he went back and began to pull the screen door open.

Suddenly Cheryl noticed her next-door neighbor come out of his house and start walking toward the street. He was probably going to his mailbox. She realized that if the man on her front porch meant her harm, he wouldn't do anything with Mr. Gruber watching. Taking a deep breath, Cheryl stepped out from around the house and snuck up behind the figure standing at the door.

"Who are you, and what do you want?" she said loudly.

The man jumped and whirled around, almost dropping something in his hands. At the same time, Mr. Gruber abandoned his trip to the mailbox and turned to see what was going on.

"I said, what are you doing here?" Cheryl said again as loudly as she could so Mr. Gruber could hear. "What do you want?"

She moved closer and found herself staring into the face of a young man whose eyes were as wide as saucers.

"I . . . I'm from the Honey Bee. I mean, I work there. Kathy said you ordered some c–cookies but you f–forgot to pick them up." He held out a box clearly marked *Honey Bee Café* on the front.

Cheryl recognized him from one of her many trips to the restaurant. "Why didn't you ring the bell?" she asked, trying to keep the exasperation out of her voice.

"I . . . I did. I don't think it's working. That's why I tried to look in the window. To see if you were home."

Cheryl had noticed a couple of days ago that the bell wasn't working and had intended to check it out when she had time. She suddenly wished she'd taken care of it sooner.

"Is everything okay, Cheryl?" Mr. Gruber called out.

Embarrassed and wanting nothing more than to pretend she hadn't just scared the wits out of a boy who had been trying to do her a favor, she waved her hand at him. "Everything's fine, Mr. Gruber. Thank you."

She hurried up to the door and took the box from the boy who looked at her as if she were mentally unhinged.

"I'm so sorry," she said. "I didn't know who you were. I thought you might be . . ." She stopped as she realized there was no good way to finish that sentence in a way that wouldn't make her seem even more unstable. "Never mind. I really appreciate this. If you'll wait a minute, I'd like to give you something for your trouble."

The young man shook his head and backed slowly down the stairs. "No, ma'am," he said. "I . . . I need to get going." He turned and ran down the street toward his car like he was being chased by rabid dogs.

Cheryl waved once more at Mr. Gruber and tried to open the front door. Of course, it was locked. Her keys were in her purse, which was in the house. Glancing once more at her neighbor, who seemed to be extremely amused by the entire situation, she walked quickly around the side of the house and went in the back door.

She put the cookies on the kitchen counter and then leaned against it. Beau stared up at her with concern. "I know, I know," she said to him. "I'm acting like a crazy person." She shook her head as she wondered if she would be looking suspiciously at everyone until Jerry Harper was found. Her peaceful life in Sugarcreek was turning into something quite different.

Chapter Seven

Trying to forget what had happened back at the house, Cheryl got in her car and headed toward the Millers' farm. She forced herself to take a deep breath. Not only was she still tense after her surprise delivery, but she couldn't shake the nervous feeling that came with not being quite sure what to expect at an Amish meal. Following the signpost on the edge of town, she drove a couple of miles before she saw the sign for Millers' Petting Zoo. Since she was running a little early, she pulled into the parking lot. Then she got out of the car to look around. She saw all kinds of animals: pygmy goats, lambs, calves, chickens, ducks, and even miniature horses. There were more areas beyond the first big barn and the fenced pens that were visible. Large wagons with horses sat out front, waiting to take visitors on a tour of the farm and its animals. Cheryl decided that when she could, she'd come back and take the entire tour. She'd just started toward her car when she heard someone call out her name. She turned around and saw Eli, the Millers' youngest son, headed her way.

"Did you come to see our petting zoo?" he asked with a smile as he approached.

She returned his smile and nodded. "I'm on the way to your house for dinner and was curious about the maze and petting zoo."

Eli's dark hair framed a friendly face. He was a handsome young man who probably had turned more than one Amish girl's head.

"Let me give you a quick tour," he said. "You will still get to my house in plenty of time."

Cheryl glanced at her watch. She had plenty of time, so she agreed. "I love animals," she said as she followed Eli to the entrance.

"Then you will like our zoo," Eli said. "We treat our animals with respect."

"I heard that at one time the Amish didn't really have pets. Animals were seen only as livestock."

Eli paused in front of a pen with several pygmy goats. "That may be true," he said softly as he stretched his hand out toward a cute black-and-white goat that came up to him. "I believe Daed was raised that way, but Maam has a soft spot for all of God's creatures. Her gentle ways have worn him down, I think. When it turns really cold, he comes down here to make sure all the animals are warm and comfortable." He pointed to a large barn at the back of the zoo. "He has insulated the barn for their comfort." He laughed. "In the winter, when he does not put enough wood on the fire, Maam teases him. She tells him he cares more for the animals than he does for his family."

Cheryl chuckled. The Millers were such a close-knit family. She couldn't help but be a little jealous. She loved her parents and her brother, but they certainly didn't have the kind of bond the Millers did.

"Here," Eli said. "This is Domino. He loves to be petted."

Cheryl leaned down and stroked the tiny goat's head. "He's really precious. I'm afraid I'd take him home if he were mine."

Eli nodded. "Elizabeth has brought him to the house more than once. Daed scolds her for it." He grinned. "But he does not make her take him back right away. More than once I have found him sitting in the living room with Domino on his lap."

Domino rubbed his head against Cheryl's hand. Two other goats came up and began to push at each other, trying to get Eli's and Cheryl's attention.

"I think they're jealous," Cheryl said, laughing.

"Yes, I believe they are." Eli chided them for their antics, which made them try harder for attention.

After several more head rubs, Cheryl and Eli toured the rest of the zoo. Cheryl fell in love with the miniature horses and the soft lambs. Eli gave her some grain to feed the lambs. She stroked their velvety faces with one hand as they gently nuzzled her hand as they ate.

When they circled back to the parking lot, Cheryl pointed toward the corn maze. She could tell just by looking that it was clearly better organized and maintained than the Gleasons'. "I went through the maze in town," she said. "I wasn't impressed."

Eli frowned. "Maam told us you were not given a map. Although some visitors like to find their way out without it, we make sure everyone takes it with them. Just in case they have a problem. I do not wish to say anything against the Gleasons, but..." He hesitated a moment. Cheryl recalled Esther's reluctance to say anything nega-tive about the Gleasons. Eli obviously felt the same way.

"I understand," Cheryl said quickly, trying to save him from saying something that might bother his conscience.

Eli nodded. "I would be happy to let you in, but you might be late to dinner."

Cheryl shook her head. "I think I'll stay out of mazes for a while. Maybe another time?"

Eli smiled. "Anytime. You let me know when you are ready."

"Thank you. And thank you so much for showing me around. I loved it." She pulled her car keys out of her coat pocket. "I guess I'll see you at the house?"

He nodded. "As soon as I close everything down I will be home." He paused for a moment and looked down at the ground. Cheryl waited because she sensed he had something else on his mind. "I . . . I am glad you have come to Sugarcreek, Cheryl. Maam misses Mitzi, but I see she has found a friend in you. Friends are precious gifts."

Cheryl was touched by his comment and felt a wave of emo-tion wash over her. She felt blessed by her friendship with the Millers. If someone had told her a year ago that she would become close friends with an Amish family, she would have thought they'd lost their minds.

"Thank you, Eli," she said softly. "I feel the same way."

She walked back to the car, waved good-bye, and pulled back out onto the road.

As she drove toward the Millers' farmhouse, she found herself traveling alongside a lovely creek. To turn into the yard, she had to cross a charming old covered bridge that stretched over the babbling water. When she reached the other side, she discovered a huge white farm house with a wraparound porch. Next to the house were two carriages. Three horses were inside a large fenced pasture. They seemed to be watching her with interest. She parked her car near the buggies, then walked over to the fence where the horses stood. One of them, a huge black horse, extended his head to meet her. Cheryl stroked his soft muzzle and let him rest his head on her shoulder.

"Samson loves carrots," a voice said from behind her.

She turned to see Levi standing a few feet away. He held a carrot in his hand, which he gave to Cheryl.

"Thank you," she said. "He's gorgeous."

"Yes, he is. These other two characters are Methuselah and Obadiah." He pointed to another horse standing out in the pasture. "That's Sugar. His sister, Spice, is with Eli at the petting zoo. They are buggy horses. These big fellas are Morgans. Workhorses. We use them around the farm." He pointed at the carrot in Cheryl's hand. "It is easier for him when the pieces are smaller."

Cheryl snapped the carrot into three little parts. Then she put one of the pieces on her palm and held it out to Samson. His velvety muzzle tickled her hand as he gently picked up the treat.

"He's so calm and gentle," she said.

Levi smiled. "He is used to people. Samson was born on our farm, and he has become more than just a horse. He is part of our family, as are all of our horses. Daed and I named the Morgans. Esther named Sugar and Spice."

Cheryl laughed. "That sounds just like her."

Levi smiled and nodded. He handed her two more carrots, which she shared with the other Morgans who were just as serene as Samson. When they finished eating, she ran her hand down Samson's soft face. "I love horses. When I was young, I took riding lessons. Always thought I'd end up owning my own horse. But that never happened."

"You are welcome to come here any time and ride," Levi said. "Samson likes you. I think he would enjoy spending time with you."

Cheryl looked up into Levi's face and was struck by the kindness in his eyes. "I would like that, Levi. Thank you."

He nodded. "We should go inside now. Maam has been cooking up a storm. She is very happy you have agreed to share a meal with us."

"I'm honored to be invited."

Cheryl patted Samson once more and followed Levi to the front porch of the large white house. He held the door open and Cheryl stepped inside.

The main living area was roomy and comfortable looking. A large and colorful rag rug lay on the polished wood floor. A blue cloth couch sat against one wall, a lovely white lace doily across the back. Dark blue and white quilted pillows were positioned against the arms of the couch. Nearby were three beautifully carved wooden rocking chairs and two recliners that looked recently re-covered. A tall mahogany cabinet with glass doors stood in one corner of the room. It was a lovely piece, simple but beautifully made. Inside were various pieces of china and glassware. Against the other wall was a large brick fireplace where an evening fire burned brightly. The October chill dissipated in the warmth of the inviting room.

"May I take your coat?" Levi asked.

Cheryl nodded and slid her coat off, handing it to him. When he reached for it, their hands touched. Cheryl thought she saw an odd expression cross Levi's face but immediately dismissed it as her imagination.

"Ach, there you are, my friend."

Cheryl turned to see Naomi coming into the room, a wide smile on her face. She wore her usual dark blue dress, but instead of a white apron, she had on a blue kitchen apron dusted with flour and a few other stains that were probably ingredients from their upcoming meal. Cheryl was struck by the joy on her face. It was clear that Naomi was in her element—being a mother and a hostess.

"I am so glad you are here," she said. "Please come into my kitchen."

Cheryl walked into a room even larger than the living room. It was obvious the kitchen was the heart of this house. A huge wooden table sat in the middle of the room, laid out for supper. Against the wall was a long wooden sideboard loaded with food. Hanging above the table was a gas-powered lantern that lit their surroundings with a soft glow. Food bubbled in pots on top of an old-fashioned gas range, and a large white refrigerator, fueled by propane, sat near the large farm sink, framed by wooden cabinets. As Cheryl walked farther into the kitchen, she noticed a small alcove lined with shelves. The shelves held all kinds of food, including jars of preserves, fruits, and vegetables.

Esther was just taking a pan of bread out of the oven, and her sister Elizabeth was mashing potatoes in a large bowl.

"Cheryl," Esther said when she saw her. "I am so glad you are here." She came over and gave Cheryl a hug.

"Ach, Cheryl," Elizabeth said. "It is so nice to see you again."

Elizabeth was two years older than her sixteen-year-old sister, but they looked so much alike, it was hard to tell them apart. Naomi's children had dark hair like their mother, while Levi and Caleb were blond like their mother, Seth's first wife, Ruth. Cheryl had heard that Elizabeth was being courted by a local Amish boy. It was easy to believe because of her gentle beauty. She reminded Cheryl of the peaceful deer that sometimes wandered through her backyard. She had large brown doe eyes and an aura of sweetness and innocence. Esther had the same qualities, but there was a spark of playfulness about her that made her a little different than her sister.

Naomi pointed at Levi. "Please get Cheryl something to drink, Levi, and entertain her in the living room for a few minutes." She smiled at Cheryl. "We are almost ready, but there is always something that does not cook the way it is supposed to, ain't so?"

Cheryl laughed. "In my kitchen nothing cooks the way it's supposed to."

Naomi chuckled and went back to her pot on the stove.

"What would you like to drink, Cheryl?" Levi asked. "We have water, tea, and milk. But I recommend our fresh apple cider. We make it from our own apples."

"That sounds wonderful," Cheryl said. "Thank you."

He waved his arm. "Please, go out to the living room. I will be with you in a moment."

Cheryl went over to Naomi and touched her arm. "Are you sure I can't help you?"

"Ach, no." Naomi shook her head. "We are almost ready. Besides, we do not ask our guests to work."

Not wanting to risk another lecture about allowing other people to bless her, Cheryl left her friend and her daughters to their work. She went back to the living room and took a seat in one of the rocking chairs. She watched the fire, feeling more relaxed than she had in a long time. She turned her head when she heard footsteps.

"Here is your cider," Levi said, handing her a glass.

"Thank you." Cheryl took a sip and smiled as the crisp taste of apples exploded in her mouth. "That's incredible," she said. "How come we're not selling this in the store?"

Levi laughed. "You will have to ask Maam and Daed about that. Right now we only make cider for our family and our friends. I am sure Maam plans to send a jug with you this evening."

"I...I wasn't hinting for cider," she said, hoping Levi didn't think her comment was out of line.

"I know that, Cheryl," he said. "Maam told me you have a hard time accepting gifts."

Cheryl grinned. "Oh, she did, did she? Your mother is an amazing person."

"She is that." After taking a box out of a closet near the front door, Levi sat down on the hearth near the rocking chair. He handed it to Cheryl. "Here are the Bible covers we talked about. I hope they are what you expected."

She opened the box to find four incredibly beautiful covers, each one crafted and hand-tooled with care and skill. "These are just gorgeous, Levi. I don't think they'll last long in the store."

He smiled. "We will see, but I hope you are right." He stood up and removed a package from the mantel. Then he handed it to Cheryl. "This is for you."

She untied the string around the simple brown paper. Inside was the most stunning Bible cover she'd ever seen. Amid vines and flowers were the words Holy Bible. And toward the bottom she read *Cheryl*.

"Oh, Levi. It's breathtaking. But why? I mean, this must have taken a long time to make. I don't understand..."

"It was done except for the spot for your name. When I met you, I just knew the cover was meant for you. I hope you will accept it."

Cheryl blinked away tears. "Of course I will. I'll treasure it. Thank you, Levi."

He nodded, obviously pleased that the cover had touched her so much. "You are a blessing to our family, Cheryl. Both you and your aunt are so willing to sell our products. Maam and your aunt were such good friends. When she left, Maam was a little worried that she would not have the same kind of relationship with you. But she tells us that you are becoming quite close. She is grateful for your friendship, and so am I."

Cheryl felt herself blush as she gazed into his midnight blue eyes. "Your mother has made me feel welcome in Sugarcreek. I have to admit I was pretty nervous about running the shop without my aunt. But I love it here, and I feel at home. Naomi's warm welcome has a lot to do with that."

Levi smiled. "Then you are good for each other. I am very grateful."

"Grateful for what?" Esther had come into the room and stood a few feet away, smiling.

"Grateful that dinner will be ready soon," Levi said teasingly. "And grateful Maam is cooking and not you."

Esther put her hand on her hip and frowned at her older brother. "I made the biscuits. But if you don't want any..."

Levi held his hands up in surrender. "Well, first we must see if they are softer than bricks. If they are, I will eat one just so I will not hurt your feelings."

Cheryl laughed, amused to see that Amish brothers and sisters were just like siblings in any family.

"The food is ready," Esther said, shaking her head at her brother's antics. "I may let you have a biscuit—or I might not."

"If you do not, Cheryl will give me one of hers. Ain't so, Cheryl?"

"We'll have to see," Cheryl said, grinning. "If you behave...maybe."

Levi's eyes widened. "The women always gang up against the men. Daed will give me a roll."

Esther laughed and headed back to the kitchen. Levi stood to his feet and offered Cheryl his hand. Flustered, she took it and he helped her up from the rocking chair. For a brief second, she thought she saw something in his eyes that made her breath catch in her throat. But as quickly as she noticed it, it was gone.

CHAPTER EIGHT

Come in and sit down," Naomi called out as Cheryl entered the kitchen. Seth and the boys were already standing next to the table. They must have come in the back door. This was the first time Cheryl had seen the entire family gathered together in one place.

"Please, Cheryl. You are our guest. Will you sit here?" Naomi pointed to a chair on one side of the table.

Cheryl sat down, feeling a little uncomfortable as the family waited for her. But as soon as she slipped into her seat, everyone else took their place at the table. Naomi sat at one end and Seth at the other. Levi, Caleb, and Eli were across from her on one side of the large table, and the girls, Elizabeth and Esther, were seated on either side of her. Cheryl nodded at Eli, and he smiled at her.

There was silence at the table, and Cheryl looked at Seth. A rather stern-looking man with a full beard, he was hard to read. He had endured the death of a wife and the loss of a daughter who had turned her back on the Amish ways that were so important to him. These disappointments must surely have changed him some.

"Let us pray," he said.

Cheryl bowed her head with the rest of the family and waited for Seth to speak. But there was only silence. She opened one eye to observe the family. Were they waiting for her to pray? Was she committing some kind of Amish faux pas? Not sure what to do, she just sat there. Suddenly, all at once, Seth exhaled and raised his head, followed by the rest of the family. Then he reached out for the platter of fried chicken.

"This looks good enough to eat, Wife," he said.

Cheryl caught the twinkle in his eye and felt a little more relaxed. No one seemed to be the least bit uncomfortable. Obviously the Amish liked to pray silently, something she wished her aunt would have shared with her. Someday her discomfort might make a humorous story, but tonight Cheryl was just relieved she hadn't launched into a prayer and embarrassed herself.

The family exchanged small talk about their day as each bowl or plate was passed around the table. It wasn't long until Cheryl's plate was full. There was crispy fried chicken, fluffy mashed potatoes, and thick gravy swimming with pieces of chicken. She also spooned small helpings of creamed spinach, fried okra, and sliced tomatoes onto the very small empty spots on her plate. Cheryl was certain all the vegetables had come from Naomi's garden.

When the biscuits came by, she took one and put it on a smaller plate next to her larger one. Then came butter and strawberry jam. By the time Cheryl had helped herself to everything on the table, she was shocked by how much food sat in front of her. Would she ever be able to eat all of it? She watched the rest of the family attack their food with gusto. It was a wonder they all stayed so slim. If she ate as much as they seemed to, Cheryl would have to run five miles a day to work off the excess weight.

"Do you not like your food, Cheryl?"

She looked up to see Naomi staring at her.

"It's wonderful," she replied sheepishly. "I'm just wondering if my eyes were bigger than my stomach."

Naomi laughed, and the rest of the family joined in.

"The Amish take their meals very seriously," Levi said. "Perhaps you have heard this proverb? 'The family that eats together grows together.'"

"Levi Miller!" Naomi said. "You know that is not how it goes." She looked at Cheryl, a hint of a smile playing at the corners of her mouth. "The saying is: 'The family that works together grows together.' I am afraid my son likes to make jokes."

Levi winked at Cheryl. "But Maam, is it not true that a family that eats a lot will certainly grow . . . fat together?"

Naomi broke out in laughter, and her family joined in.

"Well, I'll do the best I can," Cheryl said, "but if I ate like this every night, I'd have to be rolled to work each day."

Naomi giggled. "I doubt that will happen. Amish food will only make you strong and healthy. Ain't so, Husband?"

Seth smiled at her. "Is so, Wife." He turned his attention to Cheryl. "Naomi tells me you have a problem and would like advice. After dinner, we will go into the living room and talk. I am hopeful we can assist you. I am sorry bad things have happened to you in our town. It is usually very quiet here."

Cheryl put down her fork. "Thank you, Seth. I'm sure that's true. I just need to be certain I don't make a mistake. The last thing I want is to do anything that will bring harm to Sugarcreek."

He nodded. "We will discuss it away from the table."

Cheryl gulped. Had she offended him? It was hard to get a handle on him. She looked to Naomi, who smiled at her reassuringly.

"So, Cheryl, did you see our corn maze on the way to the house?" she asked.

Cheryl smiled. "Yes. In fact, I stopped to look at the petting zoo and the maze. Eli was gracious enough to take me through the zoo. It was wonderful. I didn't have time to visit the maze, but I must say that it looks much different than the maze next door to the shop. Yours is so beautiful and professional looking. One of these days I'll run over during the day and go through it."

"You will be our guest," Seth said. "We maintain the maze and make certain our visitors enjoy their visit. We do not leave them to their own devices and allow our corn to mold."

"Seth," Naomi said quietly. "Let us not speak ill of others. We need to believe the best of everyone."

Seth's bushy eyebrows shot up, and Cheryl wondered if he would rebuke his wife for her gentle reprimand. But instead he smiled. "Ja, you are right, Wife. Thank you."

Cheryl asked the family some questions about their petting zoo and was happy to hear that, as Eli had told her, they were very careful with the animals, not allowing them to be mistreated.

Every animal was let out into larger pens in the evening so they could get exercise. She was touched to hear how much the children loved all their animals.

Finally, the dinner plates were cleared away. Naomi and Esther scooped pieces of pie onto dessert plates and passed one out to each person. Cheryl had never seen pie like it before.

"It is caramel pie," Caleb said, looking at Cheryl. "Maam makes the best caramel pie in the county."

Cheryl was struck by how much Caleb looked like his brother, Levi. Although Caleb was a few years younger, the men could be twins. Same blond hair and dark blue eyes.

"Ach, Caleb," Naomi said, looking embarrassed. "Unless you have tasted every piece of caramel pie in the county, you do not know if mine is the best."

Seth grunted. "I have tasted a lot of pie, Wife, and yours is always the best. I am not too proud to say I am married to the best cook in Ohio."

Naomi blushed. "Now, Husband. You will make Cheryl think I am arrogant."

Levi laughed loudly. "I do not believe anyone will ever call you arrogant, Maam. You are the most humble person I know."

"Hush," Naomi hissed at her stepson. "Fill your mouth with pie instead of words."

The children giggled as they dug into their dessert. Cheryl was so full she couldn't see how she was going to be able to swallow another bite, but a taste of the gooey, rich pie drove her to eat every last crumb.

After pouring coffee for the adults, Seth announced it was time to go into the living room. While the younger children began to clear the table, Seth nodded at Cheryl to follow him. As they entered the other room, Cheryl noticed that only Seth, Levi, and Naomi joined her. The rest of the family stayed in the kitchen.

"After clearing the table, the children have evening chores," Naomi explained. "Besides, we have decided we will not share this situation with them. We do not want them to worry."

Seth added another log to the fireplace, and Naomi lit two hurricane lamps in the room. The subtle light created a wonderful cozy atmosphere. Cheryl remembered wondering how her aunt could possibly live without electricity in Papua New Guinea, yet the Amish did it, and it certainly didn't seem like a hardship to them.

Levi took the same place on the hearth where he'd been before dinner. Cheryl sat in a rocking chair near the fire. There was a chill in the air, and the fire warmed her. Seth and Naomi were next to each other on the couch.

"Will you explain to us what your concerns are, Cheryl?" Seth said. "Naomi has told me a little, but I would like to hear from you."

Feeling a little nervous, Cheryl told him everything that had happened, beginning with her visit to the maze up until the note she'd found earlier in the day. She reached over and picked up her purse, pulling the note out. Before she could hand it to Seth, Levi jumped up and took the piece of paper from her, saving her from having to get up. Once Levi delivered it to his father, he went back to his place on the hearth and sat down.

Seth quickly read the note and frowned. Then he put it on the coffee table in front of him. "You think this man, this Jerry, is still in town?"

Cheryl shrugged. "That's just it. I have no idea. All I have is the memory of a voice and Abby's description—which helps very little."

"And this...Abby...cannot help you find her husband because she is afraid?"

Cheryl nodded. "She's threatened to leave town, but Rachel and Janie have asked her to stay. They feel it's better to deal with the situation now, while she's in a place where she has friends. I agree with them."

"Cheryl," Levi said, "have you contacted the police? It seems this would be the appropriate response."

"I agree," Seth said. "I have met Chief Twitchell, and I find him to be a decent man."

"Abby asked me not to do that," Cheryl said. "I don't really have anything to go on. A phone conversation, a note, and a vague description. Abby is afraid going to the police will backfire. Alert Jerry that she's here. Without something...concrete, I'm not sure what the chief can do to help us. I'm hopeful I can find a way to bridge the gap. Maybe locate Jerry. Or at least offer the chief some possible...suspects." Cheryl shrugged. "I know it sounds far-fetched, but I can't come up with any better ideas. That's why I'm telling you. If I'm missing something, I'm certainly willing to listen."

Seth stared into the fire for a few seconds before saying, "I understand Abby's concerns, but if this man is really dangerous, it is the job of the police to provide protection. It seems to me that you are stepping into an area you are not trained to handle properly."

"But Daed," Levi said, "if Cheryl does not have enough to give the police yet, perhaps it is wise to wait a bit."

"If I could even figure out if he's still in town," Cheryl said, "maybe it will help. Abby can't look for him, but I can. If he's gone, then Abby can hang around town until she feels safe enough and then go to a women's shelter for help. Hopefully one that Jerry has already checked out. All she needs is to get him out of her life so she can begin to put her life back together."

Seth shook his head. "I hear words like *hopefully* and *maybe*. It seems to me that this situation needs to be solved *permanently*. Abby cannot spend the rest of her life looking over her shoulder, ain't so?"

Cheryl considered Seth's words. "You're right," she said finally. "This needs to come to an end, but how can we make that happen?"

"How can we make that happen?" Seth repeated. "I am not sure we can do this. Abby will have to make some decisions to stop her husband's abuse. And hiding will not accomplish it."

"I'm not so sure she'll stay hidden much longer," Levi said. "Someone in the church has already noticed that Abby is not who she seems to be."

"You are speaking of the note found in your Bible?" Seth asked.

"Yes," Levi acknowledged.

"She's not leaving Rachel's at all now," Cheryl said, "so no one else will become suspicious."

"Husband, Abby cannot reveal herself now," Naomi said quietly. "This man is too dangerous."

"And I agree," Seth said, taking his wife's hand. "But my point is that he must be stopped here. This situation should not follow her when it is time for her to move on."

"Agreed. So how do we do that?" Levi asked.

Seth smiled. "Again the word *we*." He sighed. "I must pray about this. Right now I do not have the answer."

"I believe Cheryl is correct in saying that first we must find out if Jerry is in town," Naomi said. "If he is not, then Abby can come out of hiding. Perhaps without a climate of fear, she can begin to make some good decisions for her future."

"That makes sense," Cheryl said. "But how do we find him? Especially with the description we have. Without a picture, it could be really difficult."

"Sugarcreek is not a large town," Naomi said, "and we know most of the people here. We will begin to look for men who do not belong. Then by the process of elimination we will narrow it down to Jerry."

"And then what, Maam?" Levi asked.

Naomi took a deep breath and let it out slowly while staring at her husband. "Ach, I do not have the answer to that, Son. But once we know if he is here, and if so, where he is, then we will be one step closer to alerting Chief Twitchell. I do not know much about Englisch law, but I have to wonder if this...Jerry has crossed the line before. Usually men with violence in their hearts leave a path of destruction behind. Perhaps the police in Abby's hometown were not willing to pursue Jerry, but I am sure Chief Twitchell will not hesitate to take action. Especially if it is clear Jerry is a dangerous man."

"I hadn't thought of that, Naomi," Cheryl said. "But if his only crime is breaking a restraining order several years ago, he won't be held long, I'm afraid."

"I believe we will have to take this one step at a time," Naomi said with a sigh. "First we should try to locate Jerry. Then we will pray that Gott will guide our next steps."

Seth shook his head. "I have heard the reasons you are concerned about approaching the police prematurely, but I am not convinced your arguments are sound. I am not willing to have my family...or my friends"—he looked at Cheryl—"put into harm's way."

"It is Tuesday," Levi said. "What if we look for him until Saturday morning? At that point we will either go to the police with something that may help bring this to a close—or we will turn the situation over to them and let the chief decide the proper course of action."

Cheryl frowned. "But Abby may not want us to do that."

Seth leaned back on the couch and stared at her. "And perhaps it must be her choice in the end. But I will not allow my wife or my daughter to be put into a dangerous situation." He picked up the note from the table. "If you do not find this man or if you do not contact the police by the end of the week, Naomi and Esther will not be allowed in your store again. Or at least until the situation is resolved. I will bring in the items we sell in the Swiss Miss." He looked at Cheryl through narrowed eyes. "I am sorry, Cheryl, but this is my decision. It is not one made in haste, and it is not made with ill will toward you. I am very happy for our relationship. But it is my job as the leader of my family to protect them. And I take that responsibility very seriously."

Naomi and Cheryl looked at each other. Cheryl could see the distress on Naomi's face. She understood Seth's point of view, but she didn't want to lose Naomi's friendship.

"I do not mean to sound harsh," Seth said gently, "but this is my conclusion, and it is not open for discussion."

"I understand," Cheryl said with a sigh. "That leaves me three days to figure out who Jerry Harper is."

"No, that gives *us* three days to figure out who he is," Naomi said.

"I will not have you directly involved in this, Wife," Seth said sharply.

"Cheryl is new in town, Husband," Naomi said. "She cannot find this man without my assistance. I will simply help her to narrow down her ... suspects, but I will not put myself in harm's way."

"And I will help too," Levi said. "I can keep an eye on Maam and Cheryl. This man will not bother them if I am near."

"And what about your chores?" Seth shot back. "The farm cannot run without you."

"Eli will help me, and Elizabeth can take care of the maze for a few days. She did it when Eli had the flu." He swung his gaze to Cheryl. "I will not be able to stay in your shop all day. It is true that there are some chores that I must do, but I will be available to help you as much as I can."

Seth sighed. "I believe your mother has been reading some of your sister's books. A few of them talk about mysteries and . . . detectives. Your maam must believe she is some kind of . . . sleuth."

Levi laughed out loud. "Sleuth? Maam?"

Naomi threw her shoulders back and glared at her son. "Your mother was smart enough to raise you, ja? Perhaps she is wise enough to help her friend uncover the truth and assist a woman in distress."

The smile immediately slipped from Levi's face. "I am sorry, Maam. I did not mean to imply—"

"That I am only capable of making jams and jellies?" She sniffed and then winked at Cheryl. "No worries, my friend. We will solve this mystery. Together."

Amused by the fire in her Amish friend, Cheryl grinned at her. "Together," she echoed.

Seth shook his head. "I am not sure this is a good idea, but I will allow my wife and son to see what they can do to help you. As long as they are not put into any dangerous situations. However, you must take my warning seriously, Cheryl. My Gott-given duty is to take care of this family." He stood to his feet and held the note out toward her.

Cheryl stood up and walked over to him, taking the note from his hand. "I understand," she said. "Thank you for your willingness to help me. We'll be very careful. I won't allow anyone to be put into a precarious situation."

"I know your intentions are good," Seth said, "but I am not convinced you will be able to control every circumstance. You have until Saturday to find the answers you seek."

A short time later, Cheryl drove away from the Millers' farm with a jug of apple cider, a piece of caramel pie, and a feeling of gratefulness due to their support and friendship. However, she couldn't help but wonder if there had ever been an odder group of detectives—a single shopkeeper and an Amish mother and son.

CHAPTER NINE

Wednesday morning brought a cold rain to Sugarcreek. The dreary day matched Cheryl's mood as she lit the fire in the store's potbellied stove and prepared to open her doors. After thinking about it, she'd begun to realize that the task in front of her was rather daunting. Three days to find a man without a single clue except for a tattoo she had little to no chance of seeing. How in the world could she pull this off? She wanted to help Abby, but what if she failed? As if agreeing with her, Beau's meow sounded like a question, although she was pretty sure he was thinking more about breakfast than helping her to find Jerry Harper.

"Let's get you something to eat," she said. She'd intended to feed him before coming to the store, but she'd run behind this morning. Probably because she didn't sleep well last night. Concerns about Abby and different scenarios for finding Jerry had filled her mind until almost one in the morning. Suddenly, she heard Mitzi's voice in her head. *"Fear is just false evidence appearing real,"* she used to say. *"Listen to your heart, not to your head where the devil can whisper. Be brave and be bold. Always remember God is with you."*

Cheryl sighed. Aunt Mitzi to the rescue…again. Cheryl realized she needed to turn the situation over to God and pray for

His guidance. As soon as she made the decision, she felt a deep peace, as if God were telling her everything would be okay.

Beau meowed again. This time his tone was much more insistent.

"I know, I know," Cheryl said, smiling at the adamant feline. "If I decided to trust God last night, then I need to trust Him today as well." She laughed as Beau rubbed up against her leg. "Are you happy I decided to quit worrying, or are you trying to soften me up?"

He took off toward the backroom. Cheryl took a can of cat food out of her purse and followed him to the bathroom. After depositing the pungent food in his bowl, she grabbed her apron and headed to the door. Although she wouldn't turn the Closed sign to *Open* until ten o'clock, she unlocked the door at nine for Sugarcreek residents. They liked to get to town and pick up what they needed before the buses starting rolling in around ten or ten thirty in the morning. Cheryl did a brisk business until around nine forty-five when things began to slow down as people went home to avoid the influx of visitors. It was almost ten when Naomi and Levi came in.

"Good morning, Cheryl," Levi said with a smile. "I am sorry we could not get here sooner, but I had to help Eli get started on his chores at the farm. The animals do not like to wait for their food."

She smiled at them. "Beau's the same way. Actually, I've been pretty busy. Business just slowed down, so your timing is perfect."

They walked up to the counter. "So how do we get started?" Naomi asked. "Do you have a plan?"

Cheryl nodded. "I've made a list of a few men who have seemed...out of place. We can start there. If you know them, you can help me cross them off the list. If you will also let me know about any single men you don't know, men who are new in town, then we can also try to figure out if they might be likely candidates for Jerry Harper."

"That sounds like a reasonable idea," Levi said with a smile. "You really do have a mind for this...sleuthing."

Cheryl laughed. "I don't know about that. Frankly, it's just the process of elimination. Hopefully, when we have a list of—"

"Suspects?" Naomi said with a smile.

"Yes, suspects. Then we can begin to narrow them down to anyone who might be Jerry." Cheryl was tickled to see Naomi's interest in solving a mystery, but she knew the kind woman's heart was focused more on helping Abby Harper than it was on being an amateur detective.

At that moment, the bell over the door rang and a man walked in. He smiled at them and then began to check out the store's inventory.

Cheryl was surprised to see someone she didn't know come into the store when the Closed sign was on the door. Maybe he'd seen someone else come in and hadn't noticed. She pulled out a notebook from under the counter and grabbed a pen. "There are a couple of people I'd like to ask you about," she said, keeping her voice low. "There's a new bus driver for Annie's Amish Tours. I haven't been here that long, but I don't remember seeing him before. I got the feeling he was watching the store. Have you noticed him?"

Naomi nodded. "Ja. The previous driver was quite friendly. He used to ask me when I would have more strawberry jam. He loved it. His name was Charlie. He mentioned he was getting ready to retire, so when I saw the new man, I assumed Charlie had left. But I am not absolutely sure about this. If you wish, I will ask the new man today about Charlie. Maybe starting a conversation with him will help me to know if there is a reason to suspect him."

"As long as you talk to him while I am with you," Levi said. "Do not approach him alone, Maam."

Naomi raised an eyebrow as she stared at her son. "You may accompany me, Levi, but do not forget that I am the parent and you are the child in this relationship."

Levi blushed. "I am thirty years old. Hardly a child, Maam." He looked at Cheryl as if his mother's mild rebuke had embarrassed him. Cheryl found it charming.

"I realize that, Son, but I am hardly a child either."

Cheryl smiled. Naomi seemed like a mild-mannered woman, but she certainly had her own mind. "Getting back to my list," she said, trying to redirect her friends' attention to the matter at hand. She read two more names, but Naomi and Levi knew the men. They were longtime residents of Sugarcreek. One of them had been in the store twice lately. Cheryl had caught him watching her.

"Erick King has a roving eye," Naomi said sharply. "His wife has spoken to him about it more than once."

"He likes beautiful women," Levi said. "But he will not say or do anything inappropriate. He is too afraid of Hilda. She is built like a wrestler."

"Levi!" Naomi said impatiently. "It is not proper to talk about how women are built."

Levi rolled his eyes. "All right, Maam." He grinned at Cheryl. "I believe I will be quiet now before I get in any more trouble."

Cheryl nodded, but her attention was still on Levi's comment about "beautiful women." Was he saying he found her beautiful? As quickly as the thought came, she pushed it away. Her emotions were still tender from Lance's rejection. A compliment from a man was like medicine to her injured soul, but Levi hadn't directed the remark toward her. Cheryl was certain she was only hearing what she wanted to hear.

Naomi sniffed and turned her attention back to Cheryl. "The other fellow you mentioned is simply a rather sour man. He has always been like that. It is just his way."

Cheryl nodded. "Have either one of you met Bob Gleason's brother, Stanley? He's helping out at their maze." Cheryl was still bothered by the look that passed between Bob and Tillie when they'd talked about Stanley. Although she was fairly certain Stanley couldn't be Jerry Harper, she still wondered why the Gleasons had acted oddly when his name was mentioned.

"Brother?" Levi said, obviously not committed to his pledge of silence. He frowned. "Bob once told me he has no brothers or sisters."

"Could Stanley be Tillie's brother?" Naomi asked.

"I...I don't know," Cheryl said. "I was certain they said Stanley was Bob's brother, but maybe I misunderstood."

"Something else to follow up on," Naomi said.

"I doubt Bob remembers telling me he has no siblings," Levi said. "I will visit the maze and try to meet this Stanley. Maybe I can find out more about him."

Cheryl was about to say something when she noticed her customer approaching the counter. "Let me help this man, and I'll get back with you," Cheryl said softly. Levi and Naomi stepped away to let Cheryl tend to business. When the man came up to the register, she didn't notice anything in his hands.

"May I help you?" she asked.

The man had dark blond hair, glasses, and a goatee. He smiled at her. "Well, I'm not sure," he said. He stuck his hand out. "I'm Mike Taylor. I'm staying at the Village Inn. The bed-and-breakfast down the street?"

"Nice to meet you, Mike. I'm Cheryl. I hope you're enjoying your stay in Sugarcreek."

He nodded. "I love it here. I've spent the past thirty years in banking, but I'm looking for a new direction in life." He gazed around the shop. "I don't suppose this shop is for sale? It's charming."

"Thank you. Actually, my aunt owns it. I'm just running it for her while she's overseas."

"Well, when you talk to her, will you tell her I'm very interested? I totally understand if she's not looking to sell. If I owned this shop, I wouldn't want to let it go."

His smile seemed genuine, but Cheryl's alarm bells were going off. Could this be Jerry Harper? Was he fishing for information?

"Why don't you give me your telephone number?" Cheryl said, thinking quickly.

Mike rattled off a number, which Cheryl wrote down. "That's my cell phone. You can reach me there almost anytime. I'm going to be in town for a few days, looking around for other possibilities.

After that, I'm heading home to Loudonville. Don't want to miss Octoberfest. This place is first on my list though. If your aunt would like to talk to me, I'd love to make her a very generous offer."

"Thanks. I'll certainly keep that in mind."

Mike flashed another smile and left. Levi and Naomi stepped back up to the counter.

"Well, add another name to the list," Cheryl said.

"What makes you distrust him?" Naomi asked in a whisper.

The door opened and a regular customer came in who bought cheese every week. Cheryl greeted her but knew it would take the woman at least ten minutes to make her selections.

"He said he's interested in buying the shop," she told her friends in a low voice.

Levi frowned. "Why is that suspicious?"

"I would think anyone really interested in buying a business would ask a few questions, don't you? Like what do you sell? How much do you bring in? They'd want to see tax papers, proof that the business is profitable. He was a little too eager after only a quick look around." Cheryl sighed. "I hope he didn't overhear us."

"But maybe he felt he should gauge your interest before asking those questions," Levi said.

Cheryl thought this over. "Maybe," she said slowly. "But he's new, and he's the right age and height."

Levi nodded slowly. "We need to put him on the list. What was his name?"

"Mike Taylor. And he's staying at the Village Inn Bed-and-Breakfast."

"The owners are friends," Levi said. "I will speak to the Bakkers. See if they have noticed anything…unusual."

"Just be careful, Son," Naomi said. "We do not want this man to find out we are suspicious. Not only because we do not want to alert Jerry Harper we are looking for him, but also in case this man is innocent. I have no desire to bear false witness against another human being."

"Yes, Maam. I will tread carefully." He smiled at the women. "I will go out and gather some information for us. Perhaps we can have lunch together?"

Naomi nodded. "I have another delivery for Greta Yoder in the buggy. If we eat at their fine establishment, I can give her the jam she has requested."

Levi nodded. "I could go for one of August's meatloaf sandwiches."

August Yoder was known for his home-style cooking. Greta ran the place while August spent his time in the kitchen. Many of the Amish men teased him about it, but August took it all in stride. The restaurant was allowed to have electricity under the local Ordnung. The Amish bishops and elders recognized the need for more modern methods to operate local businesses in a town known for its tourist trade.

"And it has been too long since I had a bologna sandwich," Naomi said with a smile.

"Bologna?" Cheryl said. "What's so special about bologna?"

Naomi laughed. "This is not like the bologna you find in the store, Cheryl. August uses Yoder's Trail Bologna in his sandwiches. It is made not far from here, and it is wonderful."

"I'll take your word for it," she said with a smile. "And lunch is on me."

Naomi shook her head. "Oh no. We could not..."

Cheryl frowned and addressed the Amish woman in a somber tone. "Naomi, you should never turn down a gift. You stop the hand of God, and you rob the giver of a blessing."

Naomi's eyes widened, and she chuckled. "My words have come back to me, I see. All right. We accept your gift with thanks."

"Good."

Just then, the bus from Annie's Amish Tours rumbled down the street and parked right across from the Swiss Miss. It was a little early today. Cheryl excused herself and hurried over to the sign on the door, flipping it over.

"I have some other deliveries to make," Naomi said. "I will leave you for now, but I will be back by lunchtime."

"And I will begin my...investigation," Levi said with a grin. "What do Englischers say? We must coordinate our watches?"

Naomi looked at him with her mouth open.

His laugh was deep and throaty. "Do not worry, Maam. It is something I heard when I was in school. I am not watching spy movies behind your back."

"I should hope not," Naomi huffed. She secretly winked at Cheryl, who realized she was teasing her stepson.

Cheryl smiled as she watched them leave. Naomi climbed into her buggy and headed one way while Levi took off walking toward the maze. She was touched and honored by their friendship and their concern for her well-being.

She was relieved to see Lydia come into the store about the same time the tourists began to pour in from the bus. Today she wore her regular Amish garb. After donning her apron, Lydia jumped right in, helping to assist each customer. Even though Cheryl was concerned about some of the girl's choices, she was a hard worker and a trustworthy employee. Cheryl could certainly understand why her aunt had hired her.

"Lydia is a diamond in the rough," her aunt had said. "But her heart isn't hard like a gemstone. It's soft and easily injured. I have great love for her. I hope you will too."

Cheryl had just rung up a large order when she noticed the bus driver leaning up against the side of the vehicle. Once again, his attention seemed focused on the Swiss Miss. Cheryl turned away when another customer came up and asked a question about one of their aprons. When she walked away, Cheryl looked for the driver, but he'd disappeared. Wondering where he'd gone, she walked toward the front window and looked up and down the street. He was nowhere to be seen. Assuming he must be on the bus, she swung around and found herself staring straight into the frowning face of the bus driver.

CHAPTER TEN

"C an...can I help you?" Cheryl took several steps back, trying to calm her racing heart. Was she looking at Jerry Harper? Did he know what she was up to?

The driver's face relaxed, and he smiled. "Sorry. Didn't mean to sneak up on you like that. Just thought I'd come in and see what all the fuss is about. My passengers surely love this place."

The man had a slight twang, and Cheryl tried to place it. Abby and her husband had lived in Nebraska, but the driver sounded as if he originated from Texas. Of course, he could purposely be trying to misdirect her.

"I...I'm glad you came in," she managed to say. "Please look around. If I can help you with anything..."

"Thanks, ma'am," he drawled. "Might pick up somethin' for the wife."

As he walked away, Cheryl looked him over. The height was about right. He had brown hair, just like Jerry Harper, but Abby had said Jerry had a medium build. The bus driver had a definite potbelly. Could it be fake? She wasn't sure, but it was certainly possible.

The driver turned and caught her looking at him. Cheryl busied herself helping a small group of women looking over a display of candy. Several local Amish people, including Naomi, made different kinds of candies. Naomi's fudge was some of the best Cheryl had ever tasted. She also sold peanut brittle and toffee made by another local woman. All three types of candy were popular, not only with tourists but with the citizens of Sugarcreek. As she packaged up the women's choices, she kept her eye on the driver. He appeared to just be looking around. At the moment, he was focused on a display of Amish cookbooks.

"Excuse me."

Cheryl turned her attention to an elderly gentleman who was standing a few feet away.

"How much is this? It's not marked." He held up another Amish doll, just like the one she'd sold earlier in the week. Her anonymous friend had struck again.

"Sorry. It's twenty dollars."

He nodded. "My daughter would just love this. Thanks."

She helped the man and had just checked out the women who bought the candy when the driver came up to the register.

"I'll take this cookbook for the wife." He winked at her. "Not sure this will help her much. She sure ain't the best cook in the world, but I love her anyway." He put a small box of fudge on top of the book. "And this is for me. Nothin' I like more in the world than fudge. The wife tried to make it once." He shook his head. "Decided it should be healthy. Used beans in it." He stared at Cheryl with a perplexed look. "Beans. In fudge. Not only tasted bad, I had to eat it with a spoon. Put it in the trash when she wasn't lookin'." He sighed. "I keep prayin' she'll never try that again."

Cheryl nodded. More than anything, she wanted to see the man's arm. Would she find the identifying tattoo? But how could she get the driver to remove his jacket? Several scenarios went through her head, but all of them seemed to point to disaster.

"So you're new?" she asked. "I mean, there was another bus driver before you..."

He nodded. "Yes, ma'am. Charlie. He retired. Loved this route. It was hard for him to leave."

"How long have you been with the company?" Cheryl tried to sound nonchalant and conversational.

"Been drivin' a bus for about fifteen years in Dallas. Moved my family here about six months ago. My wife's mama lives in Canton, and she's sickly. Have to say, drivin' this bus is a lot more relaxin' than runnin' a route in Dallas. I almost feel retired." He stuck his hand out. "Howard Knisley."

Cheryl shook his hand and introduced herself. Either the man was who he said he was, or he was a pretty good actor. Frankly, she just couldn't be sure.

She rang up his selections, handed him his bag, and thanked him for his purchase. "It was nice to meet you, Howard. The merchants in Sugarcreek really appreciate the business you bring us."

He smiled and nodded. "I'm glad to hear that. Maybe one of these days you can do somethin' for me." He stared at her for a moment and then turned and walked out of the store, clutching his bag.

Startled, Cheryl watched him head back to the bus. He took up his usual stance, leaning against the side of the huge vehicle, his eyes trained on the store.

"Are you all right?" Lydia asked as she came up to the counter. "You look...funny."

Cheryl shook her head, trying to refocus her attention on the girl. "Oh. Sorry. No, my mind just wandered for a moment." She smiled at Lydia. "I'm so glad you came in when you did. I appreciate your help."

Today Lydia was wearing a simple pale blue dress, and her long black hair was in a bun, with a white prayer covering on her head. Lydia had a simple, almost classic beauty. Even though she'd looked cute in the casual clothes she'd worn yesterday, there was something almost elegant about her in her Amish outfit.

"You're welcome," she said with a smile. "I know I need to finish the inventory."

"Will you get it done today?"

She nodded. "It should only take me a couple of hours."

"Good. Let me know if you need anything."

While Lydia began to work on the inventory, Cheryl straightened the shelves, checking for any other gift items that may have been added without her knowledge, but everything looked normal. A little before noon, Esther came in just as Lydia completed her work. The two girls talked a bit, and Lydia promised to come back at three so she and Esther could go to the bookstore.

One of Sugarcreek's nicest Christian bookstores, By His Grace, was just down the street from the Swiss Miss. Run by Ray and

Marion Berryhill, it was a favorite of local residents. Although a lot of the older Amish were somewhat suspicious of fiction, many of the middle-aged women and younger girls loved the Amish-themed books that had become so popular in the last several years. Naomi had expressed some concern about the romantic elements or the stories that included characters leaving the community, but Esther had shared with Cheryl that she'd caught her mother with her nose in one of her books when she thought no one was looking.

The Berryhills, an African-American family in their late thirties, were expecting their first child. After trying unsuccessfully for years to conceive, the pregnancy was not only a surprise, but a source of great joy. The couple was very popular in Sugarcreek because of their sweet spirits and generous natures, so many residents were rejoicing along with them. Some of the Amish women had dropped off homemade baby clothes, quilts, and blankets as gifts for the little girl who was expected within the next couple of months.

By the time Naomi and Levi arrived, Cheryl was ready to go. They left the store and walked down the street to Yoder's Corner. The rain was now a light sprinkle. Naomi carried an umbrella that she and Cheryl shared.

When they reached their destination, they found there was a short wait before they could be seated due to the popularity of the Amish-run restaurant. It was not only a favorite with tourists, but residents of Sugarcreek also loved its old-fashioned charm and homey recipes. They waited about fifteen minutes before Greta,

August's wife, showed them to their table. Greta was just as stout as her husband, but only about five feet tall. August was a few inches taller, but was also rotund. Their round, friendly faces always sported a smile, and their enthusiastic dispositions made their customers feel good.

Before she left, Mitzi had taken Cheryl to Yoder's for dinner and introduced her to the couple. Greta had shaken Cheryl's hand with gusto. "I know you will enjoy our food," she'd said while patting her stomach with her other hand. "As you can see, we sample everything to make sure it is delicious." Her hearty laugh had endeared her to Cheryl. The Yoders were a great couple, and the entire town loved them.

"I will send the waitress right away," Greta said as they sat down. "Until your food comes, you must sample our new apple fritters. I will send some to your table, ja? As my gift."

"Thank you, Greta," Naomi said with a smile. "I'm sure they will be delicious. We have your raspberry jam. Do you need it now, or should I bring it in after we eat?"

Greta patted Naomi's shoulder. "You must eat first and then we will do business. We have a little left. I am hopeful we will make it through the lunch rush." She smiled at Cheryl. "Our customers love Naomi's jams and jellies. Ach, we could serve cardboard biscuits, but with Naomi's touch, everyone would eat them up as if they were manna from the heavens."

Naomi snorted. "Oh, Greta, your biscuits do not need any help from my jam. They are the best in the county, and you know it."

Greta threw her hands up in the air. "See how she is? I cannot give her a compliment without her tossing it back to me." She laughed and toddled off to take care of her next customer.

When the busy waitress finally arrived at their table, the trio was ready to order. Levi asked for a meatloaf sandwich and Naomi and Cheryl ordered the fried bologna sandwich. Cheryl was still a little skeptical, but she wasn't afraid to try new things.

"So how did your morning go?" Cheryl asked when the waitress walked away.

"I am afraid I have let you down," Naomi said. "After my deliveries I went to meet the new bus driver for Annie's. But he was not at the bus."

Cheryl shook her head. "You haven't let me down. He wasn't at the bus because he was in my store."

Levi's eyebrows shot up, and Naomi frowned.

"He came into the shop?" she said. "Why?"

Cheryl recounted her meeting with Howard Knisley. "It all seemed perfectly innocent," she said. "Until he got ready to leave."

"What happened?" Levi asked.

Cheryl repeated the strange comment the man made right before he walked out of the store.

"Something for him?" Naomi repeated. "This sounds...rather ominous."

"Maybe not," Cheryl said. "I mean, it might have been a harmless statement. He was smiling when he said it. And overall he seemed like a nice man."

Naomi considered this. "He said he was married?"

Cheryl nodded. "That doesn't mean he's telling the truth."

"Do you think he could be Jerry Harper?" Levi asked.

"He fits the description. He's the right height and his coloring matches. But his build isn't quite right."

Naomi snickered, covering her mouth with her hand. "I have seen him. He looks the way Levi will look soon if he does not stop eating so much of my caramel pie."

Levi snorted. "I do not think there is any fear of that, Maam. I work off all the food I eat." He looked at Cheryl. "Do you mean he is fat?"

She shook her head. "No, not really. He has what we refer to as a 'spare tire.'"

Levi frowned. "I do not understand. Why would he bring a tire to your store?"

Although she tried to hold it back, Cheryl burst out laughing. Naomi joined her.

"Son," Naomi said as she wiped away a tear that rolled down her cheek, "I believe this term refers to a man who is built like..." She thought for a moment. "Like Mrs. Berryhill at the bookstore."

Levi looked confused for a moment before breaking out into a wide smile. "Ach, I understand now."

Cheryl and Naomi exchanged brief looks, and Cheryl forced back a giggle.

"Could he be trying to change his appearance?" Levi asked, obviously ignoring the women's amused reaction to his confusion.

"I actually thought about that," Cheryl said. "But I couldn't stare at his stomach. You know, if we could just see his arm, it would certainly help. If he has that tattoo..."

"Getting anyone to remove their jacket in October will be difficult, ain't so?" Naomi said.

The friends stopped talking when the waitress brought their drinks, along with a plate of apple fritters. Naomi knew the Amish girl who served them, and they talked briefly with her while Cheryl tried to come up with ways to see the bus driver's arm.

"Maybe it gets hot inside the bus," she said when the waitress left. "And he'll take off his jacket."

"Maybe," Levi said doubtfully, "but what if he is wearing long sleeves? And who will go to Canton and take the trip? We can't do it. Why would Maam or I ride the bus? And he knows you."

"Well, it was a thought."

"And a good one, Cheryl," Naomi said soothingly. "We will keep working on these ideas, ja?"

"You must try one of these fritters," Naomi said. "August has outdone himself."

The three made quick work of the fritters. Cheryl couldn't believe how good they were. So light and fluffy, they almost melted in her mouth.

"Well, does anyone want to hear about my morning?" Levi asked, after eating the last fritter.

Both women nodded.

"Please, tell us, Levi," Cheryl said.

"First of all, I stopped by the corn maze and met Stanley." He looked around as if checking to see if anyone could hear him and then lowered his voice. "I would not want to call anyone a liar, but I find it hard to believe this man is related to Bob Gleason. If he is, I will eat my hat."

"Levi!" Naomi said. "What does this mean? You must always keep your word. Are you really willing to eat your hat? That cannot be good for your digestion."

"Shhhh, Maam," Levi said, grinning. "It is just an expression. I learned it from Dan Dekker at the tack and saddle store."

"I do not care where you learned it," Naomi huffed. "I will not allow my son to consume headgear. Please do not say this again."

Cheryl snorted with laughter. "I . . . I'm sorry," she managed to choke out. "But it's so funny . . . "

Naomi's rather offended expression gave in to amusement. "I know it must seem silly to you, but we teach our children that they must be people of integrity. If they say they will do something, they must follow through. They must swear to their own hurt, as the Holy Scriptures teach us. And this is certainly not something I want Levi to bind himself to."

Levi sighed loudly. "All right, Maam. No matter who Stanley is, I will not eat my hat." He winked at Cheryl who was still trying to hold back her laugher. "Now, may I continue with my story?"

"Yes, please go on," Naomi said. "As long as there will be no more talk of ingesting your clothing."

Cheryl grabbed a napkin at the table and wiped the tears from her eyes. The situation with Abby wasn't humorous, but working with two Amish amateur detectives was proving to be extremely entertaining.

"Anyway...," Levi said, drawing the word out, "Stanley does not look related in any way to Bob. The facial structure is different, the coloring, body structure." He looked at Cheryl. "Working on a farm teaches you that in most cases, the offspring of any animal has traits that relate to the parents as well as other offspring. Of course, there are rare circumstances that do not make sense, but this is the exception. Not the rule." He gazed wide-eyed at his mother, but Cheryl caught the twinkle in his eye. "Except for the time Aaron Swenson's bull broke through the fence and got to one of our cows. The calf did not look like either parent. I am convinced our cow, Maggie, had a secret boyfriend."

"Levi!" Naomi hissed. She shook her head. "My son likes to shock me when he can, but on a farm, these situations are not quite as scandalous as he would like you to think."

Levi rolled his eyes. "The point is that I have my doubts Bob and Stanley are related. Also, as I said before, I am certain Bob told me he has no brothers or sisters. Something strange is going on there, I am sure of it."

"But that would mean Bob and Tillie are in on this thing with Jerry," Cheryl said, frowning. "That doesn't make any sense."

"Could he be paying them to let him hide out as Bob's brother?" Naomi asked. "I do not like to be...judgmental about people, but the Gleasons seem to think quite highly of money."

"That's true," Cheryl said slowly, "but would they really help a man who abuses his wife? I have a hard time believing that. The

Gleasons aren't perfect people, but they seem kind-hearted. Unless they don't know the truth. I guess that could be possible."

Before Levi or Naomi could respond, the waitress brought their food. The three prayed silently, and then Cheryl took a bite of her fried bologna sandwich. It certainly didn't taste like the bologna from Cheryl's childhood. A thick slab of fried, spicy, and delicious meat accented with cheese, sweet relish, and grilled onions on a soft bun, the flavors exploded in her mouth.

"This is incredible," she said after swallowing her first bite. "It tastes more like sausage than bologna. I've never tasted anything quite like it."

Naomi smiled and nodded but didn't say anything since her mouth was full.

"Maam loves these sandwiches," Levi said. "I think they're wonderful too, but today I have a craving for a meatloaf sandwich. You must try it sometime. August makes the best meatloaf"—he shot a quick look at his mother—"except for Maam's of course."

Naomi, who had finally swallowed her food, laughed. "My son is very generous with his praise. I am afraid my meatloaf does not measure up to August's. But it is adequate, and Levi does his fair share to make sure leftovers do not last long."

After she took another bite of her sandwich and swallowed it, Cheryl went back to the previous conversation. "So you think Stanley is a possibility?" she said. "He could be Jerry?"

Levi nodded. "I believe it is possible. His eyes are not brown, but as you have said, he might be wearing contact lenses. And his hair is black, but it does not seem natural to me."

"You think it might be dyed?" Cheryl asked.

"I believe that could be the case."

"Did you actually talk to him, Son?" Naomi asked.

"A little bit," Levi said. "But he was taking money from tourists for the maze and was very busy. However,"—again he lowered his voice conspiratorially—"I saw him call someone on his cell phone. A few minutes later, Bob and Tillie showed up. And they kept an eye on me. I finally left. There was certainly something odd going on."

"Okay," Cheryl said. "So now we have two suspects. Did you find out anything about the man staying at the Village Inn?" she asked Levi.

He nodded. "I talked to Jeb and Molly Bakker. Mike Taylor checked in a few days ago, and Jeb says he seems a little strange. Asks a lot of questions about Sugarcreek—and its residents. Says he is interested in buying a business in town. But Jeb thinks he is a little too nosy."

"Was it Jeb who said this, or Molly?" Naomi asked.

Levi thought for a moment. "Now that you mention it, Maam, it was Molly who seemed the most concerned."

"Molly thinks everyone is nosy," Naomi said. "I asked her once how her tulips were thriving, and she became suspicious." Naomi smiled at Cheryl. "She enters her tulips in the county fair every year. I believe she thought I was trying to find information so I could outdo her."

"She is very mistrustful, this is true," Levi said. "But I still believe we should keep him on our list."

"We now have three good possibilities," Cheryl said. "So what do we do now?"

"I...I suppose we try to eliminate them one by one," Levi said. "If we come down to one we cannot rule out, we will talk to the police chief."

Cheryl nodded, but as her friends continued to discuss their next move, Cheryl wondered if they were just spinning their wheels. What if all three men were innocent and while they were chasing false leads, Jerry Harper found Abby? Were they helping her or actually putting her in even more danger?

Chapter Eleven

After lunch, Levi went back to the farm to make sure everything was going smoothly while Naomi stayed with Cheryl. The women barely made it into the shop when it began to rain again in earnest. It promised to be a frigid rain, fueled by a deep October chill. The Vogel brothers were playing checkers, and Beau had taken up his spot under the table, lying on Rueben's shoe. Since the brothers usually played in the morning, Cheryl wondered how they knew when to meet. There was no way Cheryl could ask them, so the answer to that question would have to remain a mystery.

A fire crackled in the stove, and the entire shop was warm and inviting. Cheryl suddenly felt overwhelmingly blessed to be exactly where she was. In Sugarcreek, running the Swiss Miss, and living among these gentle people. Once again, she thought about how a few months ago her life had been in shambles. Now, she was actually grateful Lance had called off the wedding. A scripture in Romans floated into her head. *"And we know that all things work together for good to them that love God, to them who are the called according to His purpose."* Those words had never meant more to her than they did at that moment.

"Thank You, God," she whispered.

"Did you say something?" Naomi asked.

Cheryl smiled and shook her head. "Just thanking God for bringing me to Sugarcreek."

Naomi reached over and took her arm. "I have thanked Gott for this too," she said with a smile. "I am so blessed to have a new friend. Friends are among Gott's best gifts, ain't so?"

Cheryl nodded. "Yes, they are."

Esther walked up next to her mother. "I have displayed Levi's Bible covers," she said with a shy smile. "Would you like to see them?"

Cheryl and Naomi followed her to a shelf not far from the counter. The four covers had been placed next to each other, with the price tags attached.

"They're so beautiful," Cheryl said softly. "I'm thrilled he's allowing me to sell them."

"I am happy too," Naomi said. "I do not understand why he changed his mind, but I am glad he did. I know people will cherish them."

"I agree," Cheryl said with a smile.

She went to her office to work on the books while Naomi sat out in the shop with Esther. About two o'clock, Cheryl left the office to help Esther with customers from Annie's Amish Tours. The bus came twice during the day. Once between ten and ten thirty in the morning and again around two in the afternoon. There were other tour buses that came through town, but Annie's was the only company that only came to Sugarcreek. There weren't a lot of riders today, probably due to the weather, so Esther and Cheryl took care of their customers quickly. Cheryl was grateful the driver stayed on the bus and didn't come in. After the bus pulled away, Cheryl went back to her office, finished her work, and went out front just as Lydia arrived to meet with Esther. She'd changed clothes and was back in jeans and the same blue blouse she'd worn before. Cheryl assumed the outfit was the only one she had outside of her regular clothes.

"Are you ready to go?" Lydia asked Esther as she came in.

Esther looked at Cheryl who nodded. "I will see you tomorrow," she told her with a smile.

Esther came over and gave her mother a quick hug. "I will come back and ride home with you, Maam."

"I will not leave until Cheryl does," Naomi said, "so you might as well take your time. Please give Marion my best and tell her we are praying for her and her baby."

Cheryl was silent until the two girls left the shop. "Naomi, are you staying here to...protect me?"

"Ja," she answered. "Levi and I do not feel you should be alone until the police chief is able to help us."

"Oh, Naomi." Cheryl was touched by the gesture but appalled that the two were neglecting their own lives to watch over her. "That's just not necessary. I'm surrounded by people all day. And if something concerns me, I can call the police station. It's only a couple of blocks away."

The older woman looked unconvinced. "Levi and I are very concerned about your safety. We trust that Gott watches over you, but He also gives us each other. Sometimes we feel concern because

Gott is telling us one of His children needs help." She frowned. "You have no husband to take care of you."

"But I thought Seth was worried about you spending time with me. I doubt hanging around here all day will make him happy."

"This is true. But my husband does not know what I do every minute of my life."

Cheryl shook her head. "I just won't have it. I don't want to come between the two of you." She thought for a moment. "What about this? I'll visit Chief Twitchell. Tell him about the note, but I won't mention Abby. Not yet anyway. Then if we can't find Jerry by Saturday, I'll tell him the whole story. Just like we agreed. Would that make you and Levi feel better?"

Naomi nodded slowly. "Ja, it would bring some rest to my mind. At least the chief will know there is a reason to keep a closer watch on you."

"Okay," Cheryl said, "I'll see him about the note." She shook her head. "Naomi, it's wonderful to have friends like you and your family, but I can't have you putting your lives on hold for me. And I don't want Seth to forbid you from coming here. It would break my heart."

"Even if he does, we will always be friends. I would not bring your supplies, but I will see you outside of the store."

Cheryl shrugged. "You say that, but what if Seth cuts off all contact? I don't want to take that chance." She paused for a moment as the Vogel brothers stood up from their chairs and headed out the front door.

Naomi said good-bye to them. Ben nodded, but as usual, Rueben made no eye contact with her or Cheryl.

"I do not believe Seth would do that," Naomi said as the door closed. She frowned. "What if the chief asks if you have any idea who wrote the note? What will you say?"

Cheryl pondered the question for a moment. "I'd tell him I'm not certain. Because I'm not."

The bell over the door tinkled, and Cheryl turned to see Mike Taylor walk in. Naomi and Cheryl exchanged quick glances.

"Good day, ladies," he called out. "Looks like the rain is driving away your business a little."

"It's slower than normal," Cheryl acknowledged.

"I told my wife about your shop, and she read me the riot act. Ordered me to come back and buy some things to bring home with me. Hope you don't mind if I look around a little more."

Cheryl smiled. "That's why I open the door every day."

"Of course," Mike said, laughing. "Dumb comment. Sorry."

"If there's anything I can help you with, just let me know."

"I will. Thanks."

As Mike began to inspect the displays, Naomi whispered, "He seems like a very nice man. Not the kind of man who would hurt people."

"I agree," Cheryl whispered back. "But we can't rule him out. It might be an act."

"I suppose you are right," Naomi said, keeping her voice low. "But I do not like being suspicious of people."

"I know. I don't like it either."

The two women were silent while the man carefully riffled through Cheryl's inventory. Finally, he came to the counter with a quilted apron, a cookbook, and a box of peanut brittle. "Hopefully, she'll like these." He put them on the counter and then removed his glasses, which were wet from the rain. "Guess I need windshield wipers on these things too." He set them down on the counter and reached into his pocket for his wallet. "Would you like to see my family?" He held out his wallet. A nice-looking woman and two children smiled from the photograph. The woman certainly wasn't Abby.

"Very attractive," Cheryl said.

"Thank you." Mike's wide smile showed his pride. "That shot is old. The kids are grown now, but it's always been one of my favorite pictures." He chuckled. "I tell my wife she hasn't changed a bit. She thinks I'm just saying that, but I'm quite serious." He took some cash from the wallet and handed it to Cheryl. "To me, she's always been the most beautiful girl in the world—and she always will be."

"That's lovely," Cheryl said with a sigh. "You're both very blessed."

"Yes, we are." He accepted his change and put it in his wallet. Cheryl noticed a sticker on his wallet and pointed it out.

"Oh my," he said with a chuckle. "Guess you can tell the wallet is new. My old one was falling apart."

"I've got to replace mine too," Cheryl said. "The clasp doesn't work and my change falls out inside my purse. Whenever I want change, I have to dig through everything else to find it." She pointed at the nice leather wallet. "I don't suppose you bought that in Sugarcreek, did you?"

He nodded. "At a shop called..." He hesitated a moment. "Now what was the name of that place?"

Naomi peered closely at the small sticker. "Buttons 'n' Bows. It is just a couple blocks up the street."

Mike snapped his fingers and slid his wallet back in his pocket. "That's it." He laughed. "Maybe my mind blocked it because it doesn't sound very manly to say I bought my wallet at a place called Buttons 'n' Bows."

Cheryl and Naomi both laughed.

"We won't tell anyone," Cheryl said.

Mike gave her a lopsided grin. "Thanks. I appreciate that." He took his package from Cheryl. "I don't suppose you've had time to speak to your aunt?"

Cheryl shook her head. "She's very hard to reach. It might be a while before I talk to her, but I'm pretty sure she has no interest in selling this store. I still have your number though. When I hear from her, I'll tell her about your offer."

"Thank you. That's all I can ask."

After saying good-bye, he left.

"Well, we can cross him off," Cheryl said. "He has a family, and Abby's not part of it."

Naomi nodded. "So we are down to two possibilities."

"Yeah, I guess so." Cheryl sighed.

"What is bothering you, Cheryl?"

"I just keep wondering if we're even on the right track. What if Jerry isn't in town? I hope we're not stalking innocent men."

"Ja, I am concerned about this as well."

Cheryl started to say something else when the front door opened and Levi strolled in.

"Sorry to be away so long," he said, first looking around the shop. "Everything is fine at home. The zoo and the maze are closed until the rain stops, so that has made things easier."

"Cheryl has decided to speak to the police chief now," Naomi told him.

Levi frowned and looked at Cheryl. "I thought you were going to wait until Saturday."

Cheryl quickly explained her reasons for going to the chief about the note. "That way he can keep an eye on me so you and your mother won't worry so much."

"We do not mind spending time with you," he said. "We just want to be certain you are safe."

"I understand that, Levi," Cheryl said, "and I appreciate it. But as I told your mother, I don't want to upset Seth. His first concern is for his family. As it should be. Besides, I'd feel better too, having the police aware of what's going on. It will make me feel a little safer."

Levi didn't look convinced. "I understand, but I am not sure this is prudent."

Naomi began to patiently explain why she agreed with Cheryl's conclusion. Although Levi didn't say anything, he nodded as he listened to his mother's argument.

"I do want you to feel protected, Cheryl," Levi said finally. "Of course we will support your decision. Perhaps making him aware about the note will not put Abby in any further danger. So when do you plan to speak to Chief Twitchell?"

Cheryl glanced at her watch. "I'll probably go tomorrow while Esther is here. It's a little late in the day now."

"All right," Naomi said. "I will come by in the afternoon to see how your meeting went. I can take Esther home and bring you a new batch of butter cheese."

"I'm almost out of strawberry jam too," Cheryl said. "Can you bring me a dozen more jars?"

Naomi nodded. "I will also bring some apple butter. It seems much more popular during the fall." She gave Cheryl a shy smile. "I will also be making pumpkin butter soon. It has always been a fall favorite."

"Your banana nut bread goes quickly. Will you also be making pumpkin bread?"

Naomi nodded. "I will bring you some of both."

"That sounds wonderful," Cheryl said. "I doubt it will stay on the shelf very long."

"When do you want to leave, Maam?" Levi said. "It is getting late."

"I told your sister I would stay until the shop closed."

"All right," Levi said. "Unless you want me to wait with you, I believe I will go home and start the evening chores. I'll send Eli for you and Esther."

"That is fine, Son," Naomi said with a smile. "I will see you later."

Levi said good-bye to the women and turned to go. About halfway to the door he stopped and turned around. "Ach, I almost forgot, Maam. I stopped by the *Budget* and got a copy for you." He smiled at Cheryl. "It is printed on Wednesdays and mailed to subscribers. But Maam likes to get her copy early, so I drop by and pick one up—when I remember." He reached inside his coat and pulled the folded newspaper out of an inside pocket. Then he carried it over to his mother, said good-bye once again, and left.

While Cheryl took care of the few customers that filtered in, Naomi sat down in a rocking chair next to the potbellied stove and read her paper. It was almost closing time when Naomi suddenly let out a strangled cry.

"My goodness, Naomi," Cheryl said, startled by her friend's reaction. "What's wrong?"

She got up from the rocking chair and carried her newspaper over to the counter where she opened it up and pointed to something. Cheryl moved the paper closer, looking at the spot Naomi indicated in the classified section. "William Osborne wants to sell his Jersey milk cow?" she said. "I don't understand."

"Ach, no, no," Naomi said. "Below the ad for the cow."

Cheryl's mouth dropped open as she read, "Reward offered for information leading to the whereabouts of Abby Harper. Her husband wants her to come home." It was followed by a telephone number.

CHAPTER TWELVE

Well, at least we know he's still here," Cheryl said slowly.

"Ach, I wonder. Could he have left this message because he is no longer in town?"

Cheryl considered Naomi's question. "Maybe, but obviously he thinks there's a good chance Abby might be in Sugarcreek. If he didn't, he probably wouldn't have placed the ad."

"I believe you are right," Naomi said. "So now what do we do?"

Cheryl shook her head. "I don't know. At least he doesn't seem to suspect me of knowing where she is." She pointed at the ad. "If he thought I knew something, why would he bother to buy an ad?"

Naomi was quiet for a moment. "Well, he knows you overheard him in the maze, ain't so? This means he is probably worried you might be able to identify him. But as you say, he may not have connected you to Abby. At least we can pray this is so."

"If that's true, he couldn't be any of the men we suspect."

Naomi looked confused.

"They've come into the store. If they thought I could identify them, they'd have stayed away." As soon as the words came out of her mouth, Cheryl realized there was still one man she hadn't seen.

"Naomi, I've never seen Stanley. He wasn't even there the morning I was at the corn maze."

"But he would not have a reason to hide before you overheard him, ja?"

"That's true, but he wasn't where he was supposed to be. Maybe he was in the maze."

Naomi nodded with enthusiasm. "You are right, Cheryl. I think it is time you met the elusive Stanley, ain't so?"

Cheryl hurried over to a window on the side of the store. "Sugar and grits," she said. "The maze is closed because of the rain. Tomorrow I think I'll stop by. If Stanley tries to hide from me, it will tell me he was the man in the maze."

"Not necessarily," Naomi said. "Perhaps the man is concealing something else, or maybe he is certain you did not see his face."

Cheryl nodded. "But Stanley is definitely up to something. And so are the Gleasons. We need to figure out what it is." Realizing what she'd said, she turned toward Naomi. "Sorry. I mean, *I* need to find out what he's hiding."

Naomi smiled. "Friends bear each other's burdens, Cheryl. We are in this together."

"Thank you." Cheryl appreciated Naomi's loyalty, but she felt the need to protect her. "Can we use the telephone number in the advertisement to find out who it belongs to?"

Cheryl considered Naomi's question. "If we call it, then he might be able to track the call back to us. If he doesn't suspect us of knowing about Abby now, that could change." She stared at the ad. "I don't recognize this number at all."

"Is it local?" Naomi asked.

"Yes, it's in the same area code." She sighed. "I can Google it, but it's probably a disposable, untraceable phone." She hurried over to the counter and found her notepad. Checking the phone number Mike Taylor had given her confirmed her previous conclusion that he wasn't Jerry Harper. The numbers didn't match. She closed the notepad and went back to Naomi.

Naomi was staring at her with wide eyes. "I have no idea what you just said. What is Google, and why would a phone burn?"

Cheryl patiently explained the concepts of Google and burner phones.

"So if you do not find this number on…Google…then it is probably from a number that we cannot use to find the owner?"

"Yes, exactly. I'll see what I can do, but so far Jerry's been pretty smart. I don't believe he'd leave such an obvious trail to follow."

The door opened, and Esther came in carrying a bag. New books. Naomi and Cheryl brought their conversation to a quick close.

"I am a little early, Maam," Esther said with a smile. "Are you ready to go?"

"Not until Cheryl closes," she replied, "and Eli gets here."

As soon as the words left her lips, one of the Millers' buggies pulled up outside.

"There he is," Cheryl said. "It's starting to rain harder. I'm going to close. It's almost five anyway, and no one is going to come out in this weather. Please go home before the streets flood."

"The rain is so cold, it may freeze on the roads," Esther said. "I do not want Sugar to slip carrying us home."

"Ach, you and that horse," Naomi said with a sigh. "I believe you love that horse more than your brothers and sisters."

"Well, she causes me less trouble than my brothers. Elizabeth is not a problem."

Cheryl laughed. "I have a brother too. I love him, but he can be a real pest. I understand your situation."

Esther smiled. "People think that Amish brothers must be well behaved. This is not true. They are always playing tricks on me and Elizabeth."

Naomi made a clucking sound. "You give it back as good as you get it," she said. "I remember the time you switched their underwear." She shook her head. "My poor Levi thought he had gained weight, and Eli was afraid he was wasting away."

Cheryl laughed. "Why, Esther, I can't believe it. I wouldn't have thought you capable of something like that."

Esther nodded. "I must protect myself against their shenanigans, I'm afraid. The last time I made a pie, they substituted the sugar with salt." She shuddered. "I will never forget the first bite."

"Now, that was a waste of food, and the boys were chastised for it," Naomi said. "Some tricks are not so funny."

Her tone was serious, but Cheryl saw the corners of her mouth twitch. Cheryl was touched by this tight-knit family. It was hard for her to understand how Sarah had been able to walk away from them. Cheryl valued her parents and her brother, although Matt had always been the black sheep of the family. Not that her parents didn't love him. He'd just never seemed to find his way. Eventually, he took off on his own, rarely contacting his family. Unless he needed money.

"I suppose we will be on our way if you are certain you are going home," Naomi said.

"I'm certain." Cheryl gave Naomi a hug. "Thank you for everything."

Naomi patted Cheryl's back. "It is a privilege to be your friend. I will be back tomorrow."

"You're welcome anytime, but please don't come because you feel you have to."

Naomi smiled. "I must bring you that jam and the breads you requested, ja?"

Cheryl smiled back at her. "You're right. I'd forgotten. Well, good night, ladies." She watched as the women made their way to their buggy, the rain still coming down. She went over to remove the money from the cash register.

"Oh, sugar and grits," she said with a sigh. Mike Taylor's glasses were still sitting on the counter. He'd taken them off and left them. "Hope he doesn't need them," she said to herself. She put them up to her own eyes and found that they weren't very strong. Maybe he wouldn't need them tonight. She really didn't want to drive to the inn. Finally, she decided to put them under the counter. He would probably come back tomorrow.

After placing the money in the safe in the back room, she gathered up Beau and put him in his travel crate. Then she grabbed her umbrella, locked the front door of the shop, and hurried through the rain to her car.

Although she'd told Naomi she wouldn't visit Chief Twitchell until tomorrow, the ad had rattled her more than she'd admitted. Her resolve to go right home melted a bit. "Might as well see if he's in," she told Beau who seemed more concerned about the drops of rain on his fur than anything she had to say. Cheryl laughed at his offended expression. "You'll be fine," she said. "It's just water." Although her words didn't seem to calm the insulted feline, she knew he'd be all right in the car while she visited with the chief.

It took her a few minutes to find the station, but when she did, she parked in front of the building, locked her car, and jogged inside, trying to keep dry. She realized as she opened the door that Chief Twitchell might not even be there. It would have been prudent to call first and check his schedule.

When she walked into the station, she found a woman with dark frizzy hair and large black glasses sitting behind a desk. She gave Cheryl a rather reserved smile.

"May I help you?" she asked.

"I'm wondering if Chief Twitchell is in?"

The woman's smile turned to a frown, and Cheryl realized that asking directly for the chief might have been a mistake.

"May I ask what this is concerning?" the woman said.

Cheryl stepped up closer to the desk. "I...I'm Cheryl Cooper. I'm running the Swiss Miss while my aunt Mitzi is overseas..."

At the mention of Mitzi's name, the woman's entire demeanor changed from one of wariness to one of warmth.

"Mitzi told me you were going to be watching things for her while she was doing missions. Where is she again?"

"She's in Papua New Guinea."

The woman snapped her fingers. "That's right. Now I remember." She stood up, came around the desk, and held out her hand. "I'm Delores Delgado. I'm the receptionist slash girl Friday for everyone around here. If you call for help, you'll most likely get me. I'm happy to meet you."

"I'm happy to meet you too," Cheryl said, shaking the kind woman's hand.

"The chief is still here. Let me see if he has a free minute." She pointed at a line of chairs against the wall. "Have a seat. I'll be right back."

Cheryl sat down and waited while Delores went through a frosted glass door with the words *Sugarcreek Police Department* painted on the top half. Underneath that, someone had painted *Chief Sam Twitchell*. Cheryl could hear voices coming from behind the door. A minute or two later, Delores came back.

"Go on back," she said with a smile. "He's in the first office on the right."

After thanking Delores, Cheryl followed her instruction and knocked on the door she'd indicated.

"Come on in," a deep male voice called out.

Cheryl entered a simple room with a rather worn desk, filing cabinets, a beat-up book case, and two old stuffed vinyl chairs covered in a rather revolting shade of green. Cheryl could tell by the files piled on his desk that this office belonged to a man concerned less with aesthetics and more with getting the job done. It reminded her of her father's old office at the church where he had served while she and Matthew were growing up.

"George Cooper!" her mother used to say. "What will people think if they see your office? At least throw your candy wrappers in the trash!"

Ginny Cooper was a southern belle, pulled up from her roots and planted in Ohio when she decided to marry a gawky northern boy with dreams of being the next Billy Graham. The two of them seemed to fit together to make one perfect person. Cheryl wondered more than once if she would ever find what they had.

"Are you Chief Twitchell?" Cheryl asked the man sitting behind the desk.

"Yes, ma'am. What can I do for you?"

Sam Twitchell was around forty-five with salt-and-pepper hair and a rather long nose that appeared to take up most of the space on his face. He reminded Cheryl of the man who had played the scarecrow in the *Wizard of Oz* movie.

Cheryl quickly introduced herself.

"Yes, ma'am," he said with a smile. "Mitzi told me all about you. I've been meanin' to drop by and say hello, but things have been a little busy around here. Glad to finally meet you." He motioned to one of the pukey green vinyl chairs.

"I won't take too much of your time," Cheryl said, gingerly lowering herself into one of the old chairs after checking it for cleanliness.

He waved his hand at her. "I've got plenty of time. My wife doesn't get dinner ready until around seven." He grinned. "We used to eat at six, but with me bein' so late all the time, she changed it. Now I make it home on time almost every night." He winked conspiratorially. "Trust me. The way my wife cooks, eatin' it hot is a lot better than eatin' it cold." Although he sounded as if he were kidding, the look on his face showed something else. "Now," he said, "what can I help you with?"

Cheryl took a deep breath, reached into her purse, and pulled out the note she'd found in her store. She handed it to the chief who took it from her. He read it and frowned.

"Do you know who sent this?"

Cheryl shook her head. "I have no idea, but I think it's connected to something I overheard in the Gleasons' corn maze."

"And just what did you hear?" the chief asked.

Cheryl quickly recounted her visit and the strange phone conversation she'd been witness to. "I think this note must have come from the man in the maze, but I can't prove it. I didn't see his face."

The chief handed the note back to Cheryl. "I'm not sure what I can do," he said. "I can't very well run around town askin' everyone if they wrote that note."

Cheryl nodded. "I completely understand that, Chief. I'm only telling you because..."

"You're feelin' a little unsafe?"

"Well, yes. But I'm a little more concerned about the woman he was talking about. I know the police department in Sugarcreek is small, but I just felt that if you knew about this you could...I don't know, keep your eyes open for any strange man in town."

The chief smiled. "Actually, there are a lot of strange men in this town, but I understand what you're asking."

"He seems to be looking for a woman. A woman he wants to hurt."

The chief stood up. "I'm glad you came to me, Miss Cooper. I take any threat to a woman very seriously."

Cheryl stood to her feet. "Thank you, Chief. I know it's not much to go on..."

"But it's better I know about it than to let something happen we could have prevented." He rubbed his chin. "I wonder if I could keep that note? I'm not sure it will help, but at least I'd have a chance to compare the handwriting in case anything pops up."

Cheryl handed the note back. She felt a little unsure about letting it go, but she certainly wasn't doing anything with it. Better to give it to someone who might really be able to help. She liked the chief and wanted to tell him everything about Abby and Jerry Harper. But she just couldn't do it. Not without Abby's permission. Cheryl had to wonder if meeting Chief Twitchell would change Abby's mind about talking to the police. There was a strength and confidence about the chief that elicited a feeling of trust.

The chief came around his desk and held the door open for her. "Glad you came to me, Miss Cooper. If anything else happens— anything that worries you, please call me right away, okay?"

"I will," she said with a smile. "And please. It's Cheryl."

"Thanks, Cheryl." He shook her hand one more time, and Cheryl left the station feeling good about her decision to talk to him.

She got in her car and checked on Beau. He seemed to have calmed down from his brief shower. Since it was still raining,

Cheryl was certain he would be offended again by the time they got inside the house. She could park in the small detached garage behind the house, but she'd get just as wet running from there to the kitchen door.

Cheryl stopped by the Honey Bee and picked up a grilled ham, goat cheese, and fig sandwich, along with a cup of broccoli and cheese soup for dinner. As she ran for the car, trying to stay dry, she noticed a man standing across the street, staring right at her. He stood at the entrance of the Gleasons' corn maze, a dark rain poncho over his clothes, and a black ball cap pulled down low on his face.

Cheryl climbed inside her car, chilled to the bone by the icy rain. Was this the elusive Stanley? Why was he staring at her? As she drove away, she looked in her rearview mirror. Sure enough, he had walked to the edge of the road and was watching her car. The chill she felt as she drove home was certainly due to more than just the weather.

CHAPTER THIRTEEN

The next morning Cheryl woke up with an idea. She hurried around as quickly as she could, grabbed Beau, and headed to work, praying the rain would continue. Sure enough it was still falling, and the weather forecaster on her aunt's little TV had predicted rain throughout the day.

"Dear God," she prayed as she drove to work, "if you could just keep it coming, I have an idea that might help us find Jerry Harper."

By the time she pulled up to the Swiss Miss, she'd talked herself out of her idea more than once. When she opened the front door, she wasn't sure whether she would follow through or not.

Around ten fifteen the bus from Annie's Tours parked across the street. At the same moment, Levi pulled up in his buggy with Naomi safely seated beside him. Levi helped his mother out and then grabbed a large box from the back of the buggy.

"Gut morning," Naomi said as they came inside. "I have your order."

Levi put the box on the counter, and Cheryl motioned to them to come closer to her. She explained her plan, keeping her voice low even though no one else was in the shop. Although Levi looked a little skeptical, Naomi's head bobbed up and down.

"I think it will work," she said, "but I believe you should allow me to do it."

"No, Maam," Levi said sharply. "You might catch your death of cold."

Naomi pulled herself up to her full five-feet-two-inch height and puffed out her chest. "I may be a little older than Cheryl, but I am not an old woman."

"Why do you think you are better suited for this...this performance than Cheryl?" Levi asked, frowning.

Naomi sighed. "Because...because...an Amish mother may elicit more compassion than a young energetic woman."

Cheryl laughed. "Look, you two. It doesn't matter. I'm doing this, not you, Naomi. I appreciate your willingness to help, but it's my idea, and my choice. When we get inside, you can help me then."

She went over to the candy display and grabbed a box of fudge. After putting the box on the counter, she squared her shoulders and took a deep breath. "Pray for me," she said. Then she sprinted out the door, running as fast as she could to the bus. She splashed through puddles of water as the rain poured down, soaking through her clothing and running down her face, making it hard to see. She looked up to find Howard staring at her through the driver's side window. When she rounded the front of the bus, he quickly opened the door so she could climb inside.

"Howard, I'm so sorry to bother you, but I have something for you in the shop. I was afraid to bring it out in the rain. I hoped you'd come inside and get it."

He looked at her like she'd lost her mind. "Where's your coat? You're soaked to the skin."

She shook her head. "I know. I can't believe I forgot to grab it when I ran out here. I didn't realize it was raining so hard."

He looked at her rather suspiciously. "What do you have for me?"

She smiled. "There was a problem with one of my orders. I have an extra box of fudge. I remembered how much you like it. If you'll come in and get it, it's yours."

He frowned at her. "Couldn't you have brought it with you?"

Cheryl laughed. "You know, that probably would have made more sense, but I didn't want to get it wet."

Howard looked out the window. "It's raining pretty hard. Can't I get it later? Maybe the rain will stop by the time I come back this afternoon."

Cheryl thought quickly. What could she say that wasn't a lie? "I...I can't guarantee it will be there. Naomi Miller is in the shop right now, and her son Levi loves candy. If they ask me for it..."

"Okay, okay," he said, "I'll come and get it now."

Cheryl watched as he grabbed an umbrella from a spot next to his seat. She crossed her mental fingers. Hopefully, Howard was a gentleman. If not, she was out a box of fudge—and she wouldn't be any closer to finding Jerry Harper.

Howard pulled the lever that opened the bus door. Then they both stepped out into the rain. For a moment, Cheryl wondered if her plan would work. Howard looked at her, hesitating a moment. Then with a sigh, he handed her his umbrella. She thanked him and took it. As they started toward the shop, Howard began to run ahead. Cheryl pretended to stumble, cried out, and fell to the ground. Howard stopped for a moment and looked behind him. Although he didn't look happy about it, he turned around and came back to where Cheryl lay on the muddy ground. He bent down to help her to her feet. Cheryl held on to him, walking as slowly as she could. By the time they reached the front door, Howard and Cheryl were drenched from head to toe.

Thankfully, there were no customers in the Swiss Miss. The very small crowd on the bus had gone into the Honey Bee since it was right by the bus door. Crossing the street and getting soaked by the icy rain didn't seem to be a popular option.

Cheryl shook off the umbrella on the front porch and followed Howard inside. He was shaking with the cold.

"You poor man," she said. "Give me your coat. I'll dry it for you."

"Th–that's okay," he said, shivering. "I . . . I'll just get my candy and go."

"Ach, you will not go back out in that freezing rain," Naomi said, her tone motherly and authoritative. As if reacting on instinct, Howard removed his coat and handed it to her. Naomi grabbed one of the chairs usually at the checkers table, pulled it near the potbellied stove, and draped the coat over the chair so that the warming fire could dry it.

Cheryl tried not to stare at Howard's right arm, but she couldn't help it. Unfortunately, she couldn't see through his long-sleeved shirt. Howard's jacket had kept his shirt dry, even though his pants and shoes were wet.

"We should dry the rest of your clothes," Cheryl said through chattering teeth. "You can remove them in my office and wait for them to dry."

Levi's eyebrows shot up, and he stared at Cheryl.

"Uh, no thanks. I'll just take that candy now if you don't mind." She noticed he looked rather agitated.

Determined to see her plan work, Cheryl tried to come up with something quickly. "At least sit down and have a cup of coffee while your coat dries," she said with a smile, trying to tone down the note of hysteria in her voice. "I owe you that much for helping me. I'm not usually such a klutz. Thank you so much."

After a brief hesitation, he nodded. "You're welcome. I...I guess I could use some coffee." Howard lowered himself down into the other chair at the checkers table.

Cheryl smiled at him and hurried to the back room before he could change his mind. First she took a towel from the rack next to the sink in the bathroom and dried herself the best she could. Then she grabbed some jeans and a sweatshirt she wore when she cleaned the shop. Thankfully, she'd just washed them. Her cold, wet clothes made her shiver, so pulling them off and putting on the dry clothes felt wonderful. She couldn't help but feel a little guilty about Howard. He had to be miserable. For a few seconds, Cheryl wondered if her entire plan was just a really terrible idea. What if Howard was innocent? Was she harassing the poor man for no reason? She poured a cup of coffee and then made a fast decision. Wrong or right, this might be the only time she could get to see the one thing that could prove Howard was Jerry Harper.

Abby's safety was at stake. She went into the bathroom, poured some of the coffee out, and added some cold water. After taking a deep breath, she faked a calmness she didn't feel. Then she carried the coffee toward the shivering man who looked at her hopefully.

Cheryl caught the expressions on the faces of her Amish friends a moment before she pretended to trip on the rag rug in the middle of the floor. The look of horror on their faces almost made her rethink her plan, but determination and panic propelled her forward.

The entire thing was over in seconds, but to Cheryl it felt as if it happened in slow motion. The pretend trip, the stumble, and the coffee flying out of her hand, hitting Howard's right arm. Cheryl heard Naomi's high-pitched shriek, but decided not to look at her.

"Oh, Howard, I am so sorry," Cheryl said, staring at the shocked bus driver who was dripping with lukewarm coffee.

"Ach, have you been burned?" Naomi flew to his side, the mothering side of her coming to the surface once again.

Howard's eyes mirrored surprise and horror. "No...no. I'm fine." He stood up. "Maybe I should be going..."

For some reason Cheryl couldn't understand, Levi turned and walked to the office, closing the door behind him.

"I am so, so sorry," Cheryl said again. This time she didn't have to act. She really was sorry for the poor man—if he wasn't Jerry Harper. "Give me your shirt, I'll take it to the back and wash it out so it won't stain."

At first she was afraid he was going to argue with her, but a look of resignation signaled his final surrender. Trying to soothe his ruffled feathers a bit, she walked over to the counter, picked up the box of fudge and brought it to him.

"Here. I'll get you a new cup of coffee, and you can have some candy while you wait for your shirt."

His eyes widened and sputtered incoherently for a moment. Cheryl was afraid he might be having a stroke. Eventually, she realized he was begging her not to bring him any more coffee.

"Okay," she said, giving him a reassuring smile. "Now if you'll hand me your shirt..."

Howard put the box of candy down on the table next to him, stood up, and began to remove the wet shirt. Cheryl was pretty sure she and Naomi were both holding their breaths. Underneath the long-sleeved white shirt, Howard wore a sleeveless T-shirt. And over his right arm was a huge bandage.

Stunned, Cheryl took the shirt from the nonplussed bus driver and headed to the office, not sure what to do. Was he trying to hide the tattoo? Did this prove he was Jerry? Or had everything she'd done added up to... nothing?

When she opened the door to her office, she found Levi slumped over her desk. At first she thought he was crying, but when he looked up, she realized he was shaking with laughter.

"What is wrong with you?" she hissed.

He wiped his eyes. "What is wrong with me?" he echoed. "You assaulted that man. He never stood a chance. I have never seen... anything like that." He began to laugh again.

Cheryl quickly shut the door. "If you don't hush, he'll hear you." Her comment was meant to be a rebuke, but suddenly she saw everything she'd just done as if it were played back on a TV screen. She plopped down in one of the chairs by her desk and started to giggle, covering her mouth so Howard wouldn't hear her.

"As soon as you came back into the room with that cup of coffee...I knew what you planned to do," Levi said, gasping for air. "I wanted to stop you, but it was as if my body were frozen and I could not force words out of my mouth." He shook his head. "Perhaps in the future you could warn Maam and me if you decide to...be creative."

Something about the look on his face sent her into a fresh wave of the giggles. Finally, determined to control herself, Cheryl fought for a small measure of calm.

"I've got to rinse his shirt and get back out there." She pointed at Levi. "It would help if you'd come back. Your abrupt departure looked...odd."

Levi took a deep breath. "I will go back, but before I do, can you tell me if your...antics had any positive results?"

Cheryl told him about the bandage.

"You mean you don't have a plan for that as well? Perhaps you could just rip it off his arm. At this point, it would seem completely normal."

Levi's raised eyebrow made it clear he wasn't serious, but for just a second, Cheryl found herself wondering if there really was a way to look under the large bandage. Shaking her head, she silently rebuked herself for pushing the limits of human decency. Howard Knisley had endured enough for one day.

She got up, took the shirt into the shop, and carried it over to where the bus driver's coat was drying. She felt it, found it almost completely free of moisture, and replaced the shirt on the chair.

"Your coat is dry," she told Howard, who was chewing on a piece of Naomi's fudge. "Your shirt will be dry in a few minutes." She glanced out the window. "Your passengers are still in the Honey Bee, so you have time to wait a bit." She shook her head. "Sometimes I'm just…clumsy. Again, I'm so sorry." At least Cheryl hadn't lied. She really was rather clumsy sometimes.

Howard actually managed a smile, although Cheryl wasn't sure why. His next comment answered her question. "This is the best fudge I've ever tasted. I ate the other box at one sitting."

Naomi, who was standing near Howard, smiled. "I told him I made the fudge and would be happy to keep him supplied. After all, many of the people who come to your shop and buy my fudge are brought here by his bus, ain't so?"

Cheryl nodded. "That's very nice of you," she said. She was trying to think of a way to ask him about his bandage when she caught Naomi motioning to her behind Howard's back.

"It is the least I could do for him," she said. "Besides the… mishaps that have occurred to him today, he recently had a biopsy on his arm. There was a lump." She cocked her head toward the bandage on Howard's arm.

"Oh, I'm so sorry," Cheryl said.

Howard shrugged. "Turned out to be nothin', thank the Lord, but it sure hurts. Doc says it will heal up just fine. Wish it woulda been the other arm, though. Me bein' right handed didn't help none."

"Are you sure you wouldn't like a cup of coffee?" Cheryl said. "I'll let someone else carry it."

Again, a look of alarm colored his features. "No...no, thank you. I'd better get going." He grabbed his fudge box, stood up, and snatched his shirt with his other hand.

"I don't think that's dry yet," Cheryl said.

"It's fine. Really. Thank you. I...I need to get back to the bus."

Howard put the box of candy down and pulled on his shirt. Cheryl wanted to tell him that he had buttoned it wrong, missing the top button completely so that each subsequent button was pushed through the wrong button hole, but at this point, she wasn't brave enough to say anything that might impede his escape from the Swiss Miss—and from her. After pulling on his jacket, Howard grabbed the rest of the candy, his umbrella, and ran out of the Swiss Miss like he was trying to qualify for the hundred-yard dash.

"Well, that was an abysmal failure," Cheryl said as she watched Howard sprint for safety.

She turned to find Levi and Naomi doubled over with laugher. Naomi was actually hugging herself.

"It wasn't that funny," Cheryl said, trying not to sound slightly offended. But just like she had in her office with Levi, seeing her two friends' amusement made her laugh too. She slumped down in the chair Howard had just vacated and chuckled along with Levi and Naomi.

"That poor, pitiful man," Naomi said between gasps. "He ran out of here like the devil was on his tail." She sat down in the other chair. "Ach, Cheryl. I am not sure we are cut out for this...sleuthing."

Cheryl shook her head. "Oh my. I just wanted to see his upper arm. I didn't mean to terrify him."

Levi grinned. "On a positive note, if he is Jerry Harper, he will probably leave town now."

Cheryl shrugged. "I don't think he's Jerry."

"And why do you say that?" Naomi asked. "I find it quite a coincidence that he has covered his right arm. Perhaps he is trying to hide his tattoo?"

"Well, I guess it's possible," Cheryl said. "But with his shirt off, it was pretty obvious that his spare tire," she grinned at Levi when she used the term, "wasn't fake. If Jerry is in good shape, he can't be Howard Knisley."

"Cheryl, you mentioned that Howard said he was married?" Levi said.

"Yes, that's right.."

"Well, perhaps we can ask him if he has a picture of his wife and him. It certainly helped us to rule out the man staying at the Village Inn, ja?"

"Mike Taylor?"

Levi nodded. "I am not sure he will be willing to come anywhere near us for a while."

"But he will come near me," Naomi said firmly. "Remember, I promised to make him some fudge."

"But he won't need any for a while," Cheryl said. "And we don't have that much time."

Naomi smiled. "I would not be so sure about that."

Cheryl frowned at her. "What do you mean?"

"There are six pieces of fudge in each box, ja?"

Cheryl nodded.

"I watched that man eat five pieces while you were in the back room. He only had one left. I believe he will be happy to have more."

"I doubt Mr. Knisely will ever walk through the door of this store again," Levi said. "How will you get him to show you a picture of his family?"

Naomi squared her shoulders with determination. "I will take it to him this afternoon. When the bus comes again." She sighed. "I hope he will not feel he is under attack and quit his job."

Cheryl bit her lip to keep from laughing again. Not trusting herself, she just nodded.

"It is a good plan, Maam," Levi said with a grin. "See, you are a great sleuth after all."

Naomi laughed gently. "I think I will stick with being your maam. I am much better suited for that."

"Well, I must be off," Levi said. "Although I doubt there will be much to do today if the rain continues. The zoo and the maze will be closed."

"Before you leave, I wanted to tell you about my visit with Chief Twitchell last night."

"Oh, I thought you were going today," Naomi said.

Cheryl shrugged. "I decided to see if he was there last night, and he was." She briefly described her visit with the chief.

"I am glad he has been alerted," Naomi said. "He does not know everything, but at least he will be keeping an eye on you."

"It's going to be a very slow day. You two should go home for now. And why don't you tell Esther she can have the day off?" She nodded toward the bus that was pulling away. "Most people won't want to get out in the rain."

Naomi shook her head. "But you will be alone."

"But now I can call the sheriff if anything happens that seems suspicious."

"I do not think..."

"Come on, Maam," Levi said. "You told me you had some apple butter to make. And what about Howard's fudge? Let me take you home. I will come back later and check on Cheryl, and you will see her later."

"Well...if you will do that, son, it would make me feel better."

Levi went over and took his mother's cape from the coat rack at the front of the store. Then he draped it over her shoulders. "I will be back," he said to Cheryl. "After I check on the farm, I have some business in town. I will come by just to make sure you are okay."

"Thank you," Cheryl said.

It wasn't until Naomi and Levi left that Cheryl remembered the odd man who had stared at her from the Gleason's maze the night before. Her previous bravado lessened a bit, and she shivered. Suddenly she wasn't so certain she should have sent her friends away.

CHAPTER FOURTEEN

The rest of the day went by quietly. Cheryl ate her lunch in the office, and Beau stayed close by as if he was trying to watch over her.

She still wasn't sure about Howard, but maybe Naomi's plan would work. Not everyone carried pictures of their family in their wallets, but since Howard was on the road quite a bit, it was more likely he'd have something.

"So do you have any advice?" she asked Beau. "Anything would help."

Of course there was no answer. But he did yawn, making a little squeaking noise.

"That really doesn't add anything worthwhile, but thanks," she said with a laugh. "What would I do without you, you silly cat?"

As Cheryl began to clean up from lunch, the bell over the front door rang, so she got up and went out to see what intrepid shopper was brave enough to venture out on such a cold, rainy day. When she swung the office door open, she almost ran right into Levi.

"Ach, sorry," he said. "I was worried. No one was in the shop."

Cheryl smiled. "The bell over the door rings when someone comes in. If I'm in my office, I can hear it. Besides, I don't think Sugarcreek is a hub of criminal activity."

Levi grinned. "You are right about that. Very few things are stolen from our merchants. And when they are, it usually happens when there are tourists in town."

"That's kind of sad," Cheryl said with a sigh. "Who would come to this beautiful place and steal something?" She went over to the stool behind the counter and sat down.

"It is a question I cannot answer," Levi said. "I was raised to value honesty and integrity from a very young age. I am afraid these values are not as important in the Englisch world."

Cheryl frowned. "I was taught the same thing, Levi. And I wasn't raised Amish."

He pulled a chair over and sat down a few feet away from the counter. "Have I offended you?" he asked. "It was not my intention."

Cheryl sighed. "No, of course not. I'm just on edge. I acted like an insane person this morning. That's not me." She rolled her eyes. "I worked in a bank. I've never done anything…inappropriate." She stared at Levi, her eyes wide. "I'm the daughter of a pastor. Yet today I stalked some poor bus driver, purposely flung myself in a mud puddle, poured coffee on a man who's never done anything to hurt me…" She shook her head. "I don't even know myself anymore."

Levi shook his head. "I must disagree, Cheryl. I think you are finding yourself."

Cheryl grinned at him. "So you're saying I've discovered I have a touch of insanity?"

He laughed. "No. You are brave and funny. And you care for people. You could not turn your back on Abby. These are qualities you should embrace."

"I hadn't thought about it like that," Cheryl said slowly. "My life in Columbus was…I don't know…controlled by other people. I've always been the preacher's kid—and then I was Lance's fiancée." She noticed the confused look on Levi's face. "I was engaged…for five years. But then he decided he wasn't the kind of person who should be married."

Levi's dark blue eyes narrowed. "I believe he was right. Any man who would treat a woman like that…especially a woman like you…He is not fit to marry anyone."

Cheryl nodded. "Thank you. That's a nice thing to say."

Levi frowned. "Do you miss this man?"

"You know what? I don't." Cheryl smiled. "It's funny. When I first came to Sugarcreek, I felt so alone. Even though I haven't been here long, I already feel…" She shrugged. "Happy. At peace. I'm really glad I left Columbus. The funny thing is, if Lance hadn't dumped me, I probably wouldn't have been brave enough to come here. I'm actually kind of grateful to him."

"His name was Lance?" Levi chuckled. "That seems like a rather odd name."

"Well, he was a rather odd man." Cheryl laughed heartily at her own joke, and Levi joined in.

Just then a local couple came into the shop. They were especially fond of Naomi's apple butter and stocked up on three jars. After taking care of them, Cheryl went to the back room, poured two cups of coffee, and carried them over to where Levi waited. She handed him one and kept the other cup.

"Thank you," he said, accepting the coffee with a smile. "There is a definite fall chill in the air."

Cheryl sipped her coffee and then sat down. "In Columbus I lived in an apartment near the bank. Surrounded by buildings and parking lots. Not many trees. I love all the trees here, and the way the leaves are changing." She shrugged. "I really thought I was happy there, but now all I can think about is how much I was missing."

Levi nodded. "I love living on a farm. Having the beauty of nature all around me. I do not think I would be happy in a big city."

Cheryl studied him for a moment. "No, you wouldn't like it. Sugarcreek is like... Well, it's a little piece of heaven, isn't it? God made all this beauty for us to enjoy, and then people tore a lot of it down to put up buildings and structures that will never rival God's wonderful creation." She sighed. "I've been here two weeks, and I don't think I could ever go back to the way my life used to be. That's amazing, isn't it?"

Levi nodded. "It is amazing." He took a long drink from his coffee cup and then sat it down. "I am glad you are here, Cheryl. You are a blessing to... our family."

Cheryl smiled. "Thank you. I feel the same way."

There was a moment of silence that felt comfortable and nice. Even though Cheryl didn't want to chase the feeling away, she felt she should steer the conversation back to something that wasn't quite so personal. She took a deep breath. "So we still don't know if Howard the bus driver is really Jerry the abusive husband, but he seems innocent to me. I've been thinking. Unless his tattoo is rather small, I tend to believe his story about the bandage."

"Well, Maam will find out for certain this afternoon," Levi said. "Obviously, if he has a picture with his family, he cannot be Jerry."

Cheryl nodded. "I keep worrying that we might be barking up the wrong tree. What if none of these guys are Jerry?"

Levi sighed and put down his coffee cup. "This has occurred to me as well. Over the past two days I have spent some time talking to the owners of hotels, motels, and inns in Sugarcreek, looking for any single men who arrived it town recently. Just in case someone slipped past us."

"What a great idea, Levi," Cheryl said. "I should have thought of it."

Levi laughed. "Actually, it was Daed's idea. He has been giving this matter much thought."

"Really?" Cheryl shook her head. "I'm not sure he likes me," she said softly.

"That is not true, Cheryl. He likes you very much." Levi stared into his coffee cup. "Sometimes it is hard for Amish mothers and fathers. They try very hard to protect their families from the world while still endeavoring to walk in love with everyone. Opening a door to the wrong person can lead to pain."

"Are you talking about your sister, Sarah?"

He nodded slowly. "She met her current husband during rumspringa. And now she has nothing to do with us."

"So you didn't shun her?"

Levi shook his head. "Our church does not shun except in cases where the bishop decides someone will bring harm to the community if they are allowed to interact with us. Sarah is not shunned." He took a deep breath. "To be completely honest, I believe she is ashamed of us."

"Ashamed? Because you're Amish?"

He nodded. "Many people in the world do not understand our way of life. I realize that our community has become fodder for many works of fiction, but as far as I can tell, most of them do not realistically present the reason we live the way we do. Or how we live. I am afraid it is not as exciting as these books make it seem."

Cheryl laughed. "Yeah, if things were happening in your community the way some of these books portray, you wouldn't have much time for farming."

Levi chuckled. "Do not misunderstand me. I love my life, but most of my days are filled with work. And not very exciting work."

Cheryl stared at him for a few seconds. "Levi," she said finally, "may I ask you about rumspringa? Did you participate in this… ritual? Did it help you or hurt you?"

He smiled sadly. "I never participated in rumspringa. My mother, Ruth, had died. Daed needed me by his side. Rumspringa did not seem important at the time."

"Oh, Levi. I'm so sorry."

He shook his head. "Thank you. I miss my maam, but I have been blessed by Gott. He sent Naomi to us, and she has been such a blessing to my family. I do not think about the past. Instead I try to enjoy each day Gott has given me."

"If only more people would do that. We would all be much happier."

He smiled. "You have said a true thing, Cheryl Cooper."

Cheryl took another sip of coffee. "So what did you discover when you talked to the owners of hotels in the area?" she asked, changing the subject.

"I did not find anyone else to add to our list. Most of the visitors at this time of year are either women or older couples. There are a few families, but generally they come in the summer when there is no school. The single men who come here—who are in their fifties as Jerry is—are businessmen. Most are known to the owners of our hotels and bed-and-breakfasts. I could not find anyone that arrived during the last few weeks that fit Jerry's description. Except for Mr. Taylor, of course. And we have already determined that he cannot be Jerry."

Cheryl nodded. "So we only have two suspects. Mr. Knisley and Stanley. Frankly, Stanley is looking more and more likely." She got up and walked over to the window. It was still raining and Amazin' Corn remained closed. Although she wasn't completely convinced it was a good idea, she decided to tell Levi about the man who had been watching her when she left the store the previous night.

"I do not like that, Cheryl," Levi said. "Perhaps you should not leave the store alone until we find the man who sent you that note."

She came back over and sat down. "He didn't do anything, Levi. Just stared at me."

"Still, it makes me uncomfortable, and as the Amish say, better safe than sorry."

Cheryl laughed. "I don't think that's an Amish saying. I've heard it all my life."

Levi grinned at her. "But it is possible it came from Amish lips, ain't so?"

"Yes, I guess it is," she acknowledged, amused by his attempt at humor.

"So what will you do next?"

"I've got to meet Stanley. He seems to be hiding from me."

"I would like to go with you, Cheryl," Levi said, his tone serious. "Please. I would feel much better."

"And how will I explain you? You have the only other local corn maze. It will seem as if you are spying on them."

"Well, I am spying on him."

Cheryl laughed again. Even though their conversation was based on a serious subject, she was enjoying this rainy afternoon with Levi.

"We'll see. We'll probably have to wait until tomorrow. I doubt he'll be out there today since the maze is closed."

Levi's eyes narrowed. "Tomorrow is Friday. The last day we have to find Jerry. You must go to Chief Twitchell and tell him everything if things do not proceed the way you want them to."

Cheryl sighed. "I know I said that, but…"

"Daed will expect you to keep your word, Cheryl," Levi said. His expression matched the tone of his voice. Serious and unmovable. "And so do I."

"All right. I'll do what I said. I just hope we have something to tell him. Something that will ensure Abby's safety."

"I hope for that as well."

Cheryl noticed Annie's bus pull up across the street and told Levi. They both got up and walked toward the front window. As in the morning run, the number of passengers was light. Several went into the café, but a group of about four women with umbrellas headed straight for the Swiss Miss.

"I've got to take care of these customers," Cheryl said.

"Look, there is Maam," Levi said, pointing out the window.

Sure enough, Naomi had pulled her buggy up behind the bus. With a quick look their way, she climbed down from the buggy and headed toward the door side of the bus. Sending up a silent prayer for Naomi, Cheryl tended to the ladies who were traipsing into her store, wet and bedraggled.

By the time they left, loaded down with packages, Naomi was already inside the store. She waited over by the cheese cooler until Cheryl's customers left.

"So did you talk to Howard?" Cheryl asked her when the door closed behind her last customer.

Naomi nodded, her eyes sparkling with excitement. "I did. I gave him a new box of fudge, and I asked if he had a picture of his family."

"Just like that?" Levi asked. "It sounds a little suspicious..."

"Your maam is not a dunderhead, Levi," she said with an exasperated sigh. "I did not blurt out my question. I talked about other things first."

"Okay, Maam. I apologize," Levi said with a grin. "So what did you find out?"

"He showed me a picture of himself with his wife and daughter. He is not our man."

Cheryl sighed. "So that means..."

The three friends all stared toward the windows on the side of the room.

"Jerry Harper is probably the man calling himself Stanley," Cheryl said. "We've eliminated everyone else."

"Good work, Maam," Levi said.

"It is good work, Naomi," Cheryl said. "Sure wish I'd thought of it before I put Howard through all that ill-treatment earlier."

Naomi snorted. "I did ask him if he wanted to come in since it was chilly in the bus. It was as if I had asked him if I could set him on fire. I do not think he will be spending much time in your shop for a while, Cheryl."

"I don't blame him," she responded.

"So now what?" Levi asked.

Cheryl turned to look at them. "We all go home and pray the weather report is right. It's supposed to stop raining tomorrow. Then it's time to meet Stanley. Unless something happens that convinces me he couldn't possibly be Jerry Harper, I'll go to Chief Twitchell and tell him everything."

"Should you talk to Abby before you do that?" Naomi asked, a worried look on her face. "It is her right to know, ain't so?"

Cheryl nodded. "I think you're right." She thought for a moment and then snapped her fingers. "I'll try to take a picture of him with my phone. Then I can show it to Abby. It might help us to be certain it's him."

"That sounds like a good idea," Naomi said.

"Yes, it is," Cheryl said with a sigh. "And another idea I should have tried before forcing Howard out into the rain and pouring coffee on him. Turns out the poor man was nothing more than my guinea pig."

"I do not understand what the bus driver has to do with a rodent," Naomi said with a frown.

Levi and Cheryl laughed.

"Never mind," Levi said, giving his mother a hug. "I will explain this to you later."

"Why don't you two get going?" Cheryl said. "I'm going to close up. Tell Esther I'll need her to work her regular hours tomorrow."

"When will you leave?" Levi asked. "We can wait for you."

Cheryl smiled. "Okay. Give me a few minutes, and we'll go out together."

As she got her things together, it was as if someone were whispering something to her. Something she'd forgotten. Something she'd missed. But no matter how hard she tried to figure out what it was, she just couldn't grasp it. It was like trying to catch smoke in her fingers.

Chapter Fifteen

As promised by the weather forecaster on TV, Friday dawned sunny and warmer. Cheryl had spent the night trying to figure out what she was going to say to Stanley. She still wasn't sure. By the time she got to work and unlocked the door, she'd formulated several plans. None of them to her satisfaction.

Around nine thirty, Mike Taylor came into the shop. Cheryl smiled at him and reached under the counter for his glasses.

"I'm sorry. I probably should have brought these by the inn."

He chuckled as he came up to the counter. "Not your fault and not your responsibility. I'm just glad you have them. My wife scolds me all the time for losing my glasses. She's afraid I'll get in a wreck because I can't see well enough."

He took the glasses from Cheryl and put them on. "There we go. Much better." He glanced around the store. "I'm surprised you're open. I thought you opened at ten."

Cheryl explained about the local residents who liked to stop by early before the tourists arrived.

Mike nodded. "I totally understand. I noticed the weather drove off some visitors the past couple of days."

"Yes, it's not a lot of fun to traipse around town in the rain. Especially when it's so cold."

"Do you mind if I ask how much winter affects your business?"

Cheryl smiled. "Hard for me to say since I've only been here a couple of weeks, but my aunt sometimes changes to winter hours. I guess most of the tourist trade occurs when the weather is nicer."

"Well, that's normal, I guess." He grinned. "I'm one of those weird people who loves winter and snow."

Cheryl chuckled. "Well, I'm one of them too. Nothing cozier than sitting at home with a cup of coffee and a good book while the snow falls outside."

"A woman after my own heart."

The front door opened and Rueben came in. He went straight to the checkers table and sat down.

"Well, I'd better get going," Mike said. "I'm heading home this weekend."

"So did you find a place to buy?" Cheryl asked.

Mike frowned. "Not sure. Talked to a couple of people who might be interested in selling, but not right now." He shrugged. "But I'm not that far away. I'll be back." He hesitated for a moment. "I spoke with the folks who run the corn maze next door. They seemed to consider the idea. Of course, it would only be open a few months a year, but it might be a way to get my foot in." He shook his head. "I'd certainly want to clean it up though. Frankly, it's a mess."

Cheryl's ears perked up. "So you talked to the Gleasons?"

He nodded. "They quoted a price that was a little steep for something in that kind of shape. They'd have to lower their price for me to take the idea seriously."

"Did you happen to meet Bob's brother, Stanley?"

Mike grunted. "Yes, and he's a weird one."

"How so?"

His eyes narrowed. "Can I ask why you want to know?"

Cheryl took a deep breath. What should she tell him? They knew Mike wasn't Jerry Harper, but still...Keeping Abby's secret was important. "I think I caught him watching me the other night. He makes me a little...uncomfortable."

Mike frowned. "Why don't you speak to Bob about it?"

"You...you're right. I should do that. It's just that...well, there might be someone in town. Someone up to no good." She smiled at Mike. "Sorry I can't be more specific, but I'm wondering if Stanley might be...someone else. Not the person he seems to be."

"Wow. Can I do anything to help? Would you like me to check Stanley out a little more?"

"Thanks, Mike. I don't think so. But could you tell me why you found him...odd?"

The bell over the front door rang. Ben Vogel came in, nodded at Cheryl, and joined his brother at the checkers table. Of course, Beau took this as a sign that he was needed and ran over to the table, taking up his usual place at the Vogel brothers' feet.

Right behind Ben, Janie Henderson came into the store. When she saw Cheryl talking to Mike, she turned around and began to look over the items on the store's shelves. She turned a corner and walked away until Cheryl couldn't see her anymore. She wondered if Janie was trying to stay out of sight. Was she here to talk to her about Abby?

Mike, who didn't notice Janie, leaned over. "Between us? Bob and Tillie seem very uncomfortable around him. And he asked me some strange questions."

Cheryl's eyes widened. "Questions? About what?"

Mike shook his head. "Not about what. About whom. He was looking for someone. A woman."

"Can you remember her name?"

"No, sorry. To be honest, I wasn't paying much attention. I really didn't want to be around him anymore and kind of blew him off. Sorry."

"No problem," Cheryl said. "I appreciate you being candid with me."

"Sure. If I can do anything to help, just give me a call."

Cheryl smiled. "Thanks. I will."

Mike said good-bye and left. When the bell over the door announced his departure, Janie came out of her hiding place and hurried over to the counter. There wasn't anyone else except the Vogel brothers in the store, and they were too far away to hear her. Even so, Janie kept her voice low.

"I just wanted to stop by and thank you for helping Abby," she said. "Did you see that ad in the *Budget*?" Janie's green eyes were large with concern. Her soft voice and gentle manner belied the strength and resolve she possessed. Her reputation for handling even the most difficult horse was known by most people in

Sugarcreek. Cheryl respected what she had accomplished as a single woman.

Cheryl nodded. "But I'm not sure if that means he's in town—or if he stuck that in the paper and took off so he could search for Abby somewhere else."

"I went by the *Budget*, but they wouldn't give me the name of the person who placed the ad. I didn't tell them why I was worried. Although I'm sure they'd be supportive of Abby, there are just too many people who work there. Someone could let the information slip."

Cheryl sighed. "I understand. It's hard to know what to say, and what not to say. But I think I may know who Jerry is."

Janie's eyebrows shot up. "Really?"

Cheryl quickly told her about Stanley. "And another customer mentioned that he'd asked him about a woman. Unfortunately, he didn't remember the name Stanley mentioned. But we've pretty much narrowed it down to him." She shook her head. "Of course, we might be wrong, but there is definitely something peculiar about the guy. He's suspicious enough that we're going to look at him a little closer."

Janie reached over and grabbed Cheryl's hand. "Thank you so much, Cheryl. I really appreciate your help. You're our best chance for finding Jerry. Abby can't look for him and neither can I. Jerry's seen my picture in our old yearbook. I don't look exactly the same, but he would still recognize me." Even though no one had come into the shop, Janie looked around her again before saying, "Someone's been watching my house. I've caught him out there more than once. Dark coat and hat. Yesterday he wore a big gray rain poncho. I can't see who it is. By the time I can get to the phone, he's gone."

Cheryl felt her heart beat a little faster. "I've seen him too. I'm pretty sure that's the guy I'm talking about. He's been trying to pass himself off as Bob Gleason's brother. The problem is that we're pretty sure Bob Gleason doesn't have a brother. I can't figure out why the Gleasons are allowing him to lie about who he is."

"From what Abby's told me, he could have easily threatened them. Or he could be paying them off."

"So far, every time I try to get a close look at him, he's nowhere to be found. But I'm going over there today. I'm not going to let him get away from me again."

Janie frowned. "Please be careful. Whatever you do, don't make him suspicious."

Cheryl nodded. "I have a plan. Everything will be okay." Frankly, she sounded more sure of herself than she actually felt, but she didn't want Janie to worry. "I'm going to try to take a picture of him with my phone. Hopefully, once she sees his picture, Abby will be able to confirm that it's him."

"That's a great idea," she said.

"But what if it is Jerry? Then what?"

"Then we have to go to the police. I know what Abby says, but she doesn't know Sam Twitchell the way I do. I trust him completely. He'll figure out a way to protect her. We can't let Jerry keep this up, and Abby can't keep running."

"I agree. I've been to the chief once already."

Janie's eyebrows shot up. "You didn't tell him about Abby did you?"

"No." She told Janie about the note she'd received. "I felt that at least he should be aware that someone was making threats. That way, he might be more aware of suspicious strangers in town."

"That makes good sense." She sighed. "I've known Sam a long time. I don't think he's going to be happy when he finds out we didn't come to him immediately."

Cheryl frowned. "Janie, can Jerry be charged with anything serious now? He needs to be detained for a while so Abby can get away and find someplace safe. Someplace where he won't find her."

Janie shook her head. "That's the big question. She called the police once when he hurt her several years ago while they lived in Colorado. That's when the restraining order was issued, but it's not in effect anymore. Abby never contacted the police in the town where they lived in Nebraska because the chief was a friend of Jerry's. Abby didn't trust him to help her. If Jerry attacks Abby again, especially in another jurisdiction, he could get jail time. But we don't want him to hurt her again." She sighed. "If we could just get him locked up for a while, it could make a big difference. I have no idea how to do that though."

"Well, all I can do is try to figure out who Jerry is. After that, it's up to Chief Twitchell. This thing needs to end for good. We can't let Jerry continue to harass Abby."

Janie nodded. "I know. Abby is so afraid of him. I have to wonder if that fear has actually prolonged the process." She shrugged. "But I guess that's water under the bridge. We can only go forward from here." She looked at Cheryl quizzically. "So you're going to visit this…Stanley person this afternoon?"

"Yes, that's the plan."

"Cheryl, I appreciate everything you're doing. But please let us know first before you talk to Chief Twitchell again. No matter what you or I think Abby should do, in the end, it should be her decision."

Cheryl nodded. "I understand. That's why I didn't tell him anything about Abby. Let's just hope we can prove Stanley is actually Jerry. I'll let you know what I find out. If we can at least locate Jerry, maybe we'll have a better shot of stopping him."

Janie smiled. "This situation isn't funny, but I find it very amusing that your cohorts in this situation are an Amish mother and son."

Cheryl laughed. "I know. But they've been invaluable."

Janie nodded. "It doesn't take very long to live among the Amish before you begin to respect them. They're some of the most sincere and wonderful people I've ever known."

Cheryl nodded. "I'm learning that too."

"Well, I'll be praying that your contact with Stanley will help to bring this to an end." She frowned. "But listen, Cheryl. I want you to promise you won't put yourself in harm's way. Don't see this man alone. Take someone with you, okay?"

"I'll be careful." Frankly, she wasn't sure just who she could take with her. If Stanley, aka Jerry, got violent, she was fairly certain she wouldn't get much help from Levi or Naomi. The Amish seemed to take their belief on nonviolence very seriously.

Just then the bell over the door rang again, and an elderly couple came in.

Janie quickly excused herself and grabbed two jars of apple butter. "In case anyone's watching me, it will look as if I came here to buy something." She grinned. "Besides, I love this stuff."

Cheryl nodded and rang her up.

"I've got to get going," Janie whispered, taking the bag Cheryl offered. "But keep me updated, okay?"

"I will." Cheryl watched as Janie left, and then she busied herself helping the couple.

A little after ten, the bus from Annie's pulled up across the street, and quite a few people got off. It was a very busy morning. Around eleven, Naomi and Eli pulled up to the store. Eli helped carry some new supplies inside. Cheryl asked him to put the products in the office. Once he'd done that, he took off in the buggy, leaving his mother behind. It took some time for Cheryl to wait on all her customers so she could get a chance to talk to Naomi. When the crowd cleared, Cheryl quickly told her about Janie's visit.

"Ach, I am not sure she should have come here," Naomi said. "What if Jerry is watching?"

"Janie bought something so it would look like she came in to make a purchase."

Naomi nodded. "That sounds wise, but if he knows who she is, perhaps it is still a little risky."

"You might be right," Cheryl said. "But even if Jerry is watching her, Abby's not at her house. So as long as Janie stays away from Rachel's house, it won't help him much. When Esther gets here, I'm going over to the maze. Stanley can't possibly avoid me again. I told Janie I planned to take a picture of him on my phone so I could show Abby."

"What excuse will you use?" Naomi asked, a worried look on her face. "You do not want to alert him to your real purpose."

Cheryl shrugged. "I have no idea. I've tried and tried to figure out a good reason to meet with him. Do you have any ideas?"

Naomi stared down at the floor. "What if you go there for... business reasons? You mentioned wanting to sell our cider. Perhaps you could propose providing hot cider to the Gleasons. I would think people going through the maze would be very interested. It would certainly warm them up on a cold day."

Cheryl snapped her fingers. "That's a great idea, Naomi. I can tell him it's a business proposal. But..." She paused a moment. "I don't want to lie. I'm afraid I've already stretched the truth more than I'm comfortable with. If the Gleasons are really interested, can you provide me with enough cider to keep them stocked up?"

Naomi wrinkled her nose and grinned. "The Gleasons do not have enough business to cause us a problem. We can do it easily. We already serve cider at our maze, and we have much more business than they do."

"I didn't know that." Cheryl smiled at her. "Thanks. It's perfect. I just hope Stanley is there."

"The Gleasons go out to lunch almost every day. I will watch and tell you when they leave. Then Stanley should be there alone, ain't so?"

Cheryl nodded, but she suddenly remembered Janie's warning.

"I want you to promise you won't put yourself in harm's way. Don't see this man alone. Take someone with you, okay?"

But there wasn't anyone to take. She had no choice but to go alone. Was she being foolish? Was she walking into a dangerous situation? She thought about calling Mike Taylor. He'd offered to help her, but in the end she decided not to bother him. She was probably making too much of the situation. She'd be in public, and there would be people around. Naomi would be watching. If something happened, she'd get help. As she worked away the rest of the morning, it was hard not to wonder if she was getting ready to put herself in a really dangerous situation.

Chapter Sixteen

As soon as Esther came in at noon, Cheryl went into her office to update the books from yesterday. She was counting receipts when someone knocked on her door. Naomi walked in and closed the door behind her.

"The Gleasons have left for lunch. A man is standing at the entrance to the corn maze. I believe it is the elusive Stanley." She shook her head. "I am concerned for your safety, Cheryl. Should I go with you?"

Cheryl smiled at the idea that Naomi could offer much protection against Stanley, but she appreciated the offer. "If I didn't have this great cover story, I would be a little worried," she said, trying to reassure her friend. "But I intend to act as if I didn't realize Bob and Tillie are gone. Then I'll introduce myself and briefly tell Stanley about my idea. It will give me a chance to size him up."

"But you will not try to see his arm—the way you did with Mr. Knisley?"

Cheryl laughed. "I promise. I think terrorizing one man is enough for me. My only plan is to meet him, snap his picture without his knowing, and get out of there."

Naomi made a clucking noise. "All right, but I will be watching from the window. If I see anything that concerns me, I will contact Chief Twitchell."

"Thank you."

Cheryl was aware that a lot of Amish preferred to settle their problems inside their communities, avoiding worldly institutions. But they called on the police when they deemed it necessary. That made Cheryl feel a little better.

She took off her apron, folded it up, and put it behind the counter. Then she grabbed her coat from the rack near the front door and headed outside. The air was still moist from the rain the day before. The bright sunshine was nice, but it was still quite cold.

As she walked toward the maze, Cheryl rehearsed what she would say. Hopefully, she wouldn't say or do anything that would make the man suspicious. By the time she reached the maze, she had her speech down pat, but once again, no one was there. She waited near the entrance, wondering what to do next. After a few seconds, she heard someone whistling. Finally, a man came around the corner of the maze. He stopped in his tracks when he saw her. He was the right height, but this man had black hair. Could it be dyed? A mustache and a small beard helped hide part of his face. Cheryl didn't see anything about him that would force her to believe this man couldn't be Jerry Harper.

"Hello," she said, pasting a smile on her face as he approached. "I'm looking for Bob or Tillie. Are they available?"

The man scowled at her. "No, they're at lunch. Can I help you?"

"Maybe. I'm Cheryl Cooper. I run the Swiss Miss next door." She held out her hand.

The man hesitated a minute before shaking her hand. "I'm Stanley Gleason, Bob's brother."

"Nice to meet you. Bob told me you were visiting."

"Yes, for a while. Did you want to go through the maze?"

Cheryl shook her head. "I . . . I wanted to talk to them about a business idea. You see, one of my suppliers makes the most fabulous apple cider. I thought maybe Bob and Tillie might like to sell it here. You know, after people complete the maze. Hot cider on a chilly day might just hit the spot."

Stanley frowned. "You need to talk to Bob about that. I can't help you."

"Oh, okay." Cheryl smiled at him. "So how are things going today? Are you very busy?"

"Not yet. Maybe things will pick up this afternoon."

Cheryl rocked back and forth on her heels for a few seconds, trying to come up with something else to say. In her head, the conversation about hot cider had taken a lot longer. She took a deep breath. "So where are you from, Stanley?" she said finally. "Will you be in Sugarcreek for a while?"

A look of irritation flashed across Stanley's face. "Look, lady . . ."

"Cheryl."

"Look, Cheryl, thanks for coming over to say hello, but I really need to get back to work. Maybe we can talk some other time."

"Oh, okay." She reached into her pocket and pulled out her phone. "Sorry, I need to take this." Pretending she was answering a phone call, she snapped a quick picture of Stanley. After mumbling something inane, she slid the phone back into her coat pocket. "Why don't you come over to the store when you're off duty? We sell the most awesome fudge. I'd like to give you a box as my treat."

Stanley glared at her. "Sorry. I'm diabetic. I don't eat fudge." He looked around quickly and then swung his gaze back to Cheryl. "Thanks for coming over. Good-bye now."

Cheryl mumbled something that she hoped sounded like "good-bye" and then headed back to the store. Stanley was definitely up to something. As she stood close to him, she was pretty sure she noticed some kind of glue on his mustache.

"So what happened?" Naomi asked excitedly when Cheryl returned. "You did not speak to him very long."

Esther stood near her mother. "Is everything all right?" she asked. "Is something wrong?"

"I have not told her anything," Naomi said.

"It's up to you and Seth," Cheryl said. "But she should probably be told the truth. I don't want to put her in any kind of danger."

Esther's eyebrows shot up. "Danger? Ach, Maam, there is some kind of danger?"

Naomi patted her daughter's arm. "Not to worry, little one. Gott is watching over you. I will explain later, but right now you must concentrate on your job."

Cheryl walked over to the window, and Naomi followed her. They both kept their eyes on Stanley until Cheryl realized he was staring back at them. She quickly pulled Naomi back. "He's watching us," she whispered.

Cheryl wanted to tell Naomi about her meeting with Stanley, but Esther's presence made that difficult. Since she hadn't brought a lunch, she wanted to suggest they go across the street and get something so they could talk. But Cheryl didn't feel right about leaving Esther alone in the shop right now. She was trying to figure out what to do when Levi pulled up outside. The women watched as he grabbed a large basket from the buggy and brought it inside.

"Good morning," he said with enthusiasm. "I hope you have not eaten. I brought lunch."

"Did you raid my refrigerator, Son?" Naomi asked with a smile.

"Yes, I did. I was sure it would be all right with you."

Naomi laughed. "I was just thinking about going home and getting something. I believe you are a mind reader, Levi."

He shrugged. "It was not my mind that led me down this path. It was my stomach."

Cheryl laughed. "Let's put the food on my desk."

The bell over the door rang, and a young couple came inside. Levi took the food to the office, and Naomi followed him. Esther went to help the couple. As she was showing them a lovely quilt for a baby's bed, Cheryl noticed another Amish doll on a nearby shelf. Was that three or four now? She picked it up and brought it back to the counter. This was getting ridiculous. Who was doing this and why? And how were they placing these things on her shelves without her noticing? Cheryl sighed and put the doll under the counter. Whoever was behind it wasn't trying to hurt her; they were only cheating themselves. The items were well made. Cheryl would love to offer them in the store.

After making sure Esther didn't need her, she went back to her office. Naomi had laid out the food, along with some paper plates, cups, and plastic utensils on top of Cheryl's desk.

"My, you thought of everything, Levi," she said. "Most men wouldn't think to bring all of this."

Naomi's smile showed her pride. "Levi will make some woman a wonderful husband. He is such a hard worker. And so thoughtful."

"Hush, Maam, you embarrass me."

Esther had come into the office, and she and Cheryl laughed at the way Levi blushed at his mother's compliments.

"Maam has been trying to marry me off for a long time," he said, patting his beloved stepmother on the shoulder. "But it is not an easy job."

Naomi, who was opening the containers of food, shook her head. "Levi is waiting for the perfect woman. I have told him that all women are flawed, but he does not listen. I pray he does not wait too long."

Levi winked at Cheryl. "She told me that if I was not married by the age of thirty, no one would want me."

The smile slipped from Cheryl's face. Was that how the Millers saw her? As someone no one wanted?

Naomi seemed to realize that Levi's comment had affected her. "Ach, Cheryl," she said gently. "I was only teasing Levi when I said that. Please do not take my silly comment seriously."

Cheryl shook her head. "I won't. It isn't that." She sighed. "I always thought I'd be married by now. And have children. Life hasn't quite turned out the way I thought it would."

"And that is all right," Naomi said, coming over and putting her arm around her friend. "Gott has a plan, and His plan is much better than ours. I believe the same thing about Levi. He is not married because Gott has not brought the right woman yet. But He will. And He will do the same for you."

"I am sorry for my thoughtless words," Levi said. "Please forgive me."

Cheryl waved his apology away. "You have nothing to apologize for. It hasn't been long since my fiancé broke off our engagement. Guess I'm still a little tender."

Esther cleared her throat. "If everyone is finished apologizing to everyone now, can we eat please? I am starving."

The trio laughed at Esther's attempt to bring lightheartedness to the situation.

"Yes, now we will eat," Naomi said.

Cheryl filled her plate with cold sausages, potato salad, macaroni salad, pickled beets, and corn relish. A few customers filtered in, so she and Esther took turns waiting on them. Levi also brought a thermos of apple cider. Whenever Esther left the room, Cheryl filled Levi and Naomi in on her visit with Stanley.

"So do you think this man is Jerry?" Naomi asked.

Cheryl swallowed a bit of potato salad and nodded. "I really do. We narrowed it down to the three men. Mike Taylor has a family, so he's out. So does Howard. So Stanley's the only one left. He's definitely not who he says he is, and I'm convinced he's wearing a disguise. He really didn't like it when I started questioning him." She sighed. "I've been worried we may have been on the wrong track, but now I feel very confident that we've found him." She picked up her phone and checked the picture she'd taken. It was a little fuzzy, but it would do. "I need to show this to Abby. Have her confirm that this is Jerry."

Levi nodded. "What makes you think Stanley is wearing a disguise?"

"His hair and mustache seemed fake. Most people have different tones in their hair. His was too . . . dark. Like it had been dyed. And I could almost swear he had glue on his face around his mustache. Besides, you should have seen him. He wanted me out of there. He certainly wasn't friendly."

"Maybe he is just a sloppy eater," Levi said. "I do not see how you can tell Chief Twitchell that we suspect him because he is not sociable and has something sticky on his face."

Cheryl slumped down in her office chair. "You might be right. I just don't have a smoking gun. How can I prove he's Jerry Harper? And even if I do, is that enough to arrest him?"

She realized her Amish friends were looking at her strangely. "What?" she asked.

"I do not think we should bring guns into this . . . ," Naomi said softly.

It took Cheryl a few seconds to figure out what Naomi meant, but when it became clear, she smiled. "Oh no. There aren't any guns. It's just an expression. It means..." She thought for a moment before she realized no explanation would make sense to them. "Never mind. It just means that we don't have any real reason for the chief to detain Jerry."

"So what should we do now?" Levi asked.

Cheryl pulled up the picture on her phone again and showed it to them. "This is the only thing I have, I guess. At least we can show it to Abby. Maybe she can at least tell us if this is Jerry."

Levi shook his head. "I do not think you should go to Rachel's house now. You have probably alerted Stanley that you are suspicious of him. He might be watching you, wondering if you will lead him to Abby."

Cheryl didn't have time to answer because Esther came back into the room. As they ate and talked, Cheryl turned his comment over in her mind. He was right. She couldn't risk showing Stanley where Abby was. Was a grainy photo on a phone enough to convince the chief Abby was in danger? When Esther got up to use the bathroom, Cheryl waited until she closed the door.

"You know what? We're missing something important," she whispered to her friends. "Bob and Tillie. They know Stanley isn't Bob's brother. We need to talk to them. Ask them why they're protecting him. They might not realize who he is. How dangerous he is. If I tell them..."

"If you tell them, they might tell Jerry," Levi said. "Then he will know Abby is in town. It is too big a risk. I do not trust the Gleasons."

"If you have a better idea, I'm willing to listen," Cheryl said, unable to keep the exasperation out of her voice.

The bathroom door opened, and Esther came out. At that same moment, the bell over the front door rang. Cheryl started to respond, but Esther offered to take care of it since she was already up. When she walked out, Cheryl looked at Naomi.

Naomi shook her head. "I wish I could give you good advice, but nothing comes to mind. Perhaps this is a sign that we have gone as far as we can."

"Wait a minute," Levi said. "What about the phone number in the paper? I realize you do not want to call it because it might lead back to you, but maybe you could call from a public phone? One of us could be within earshot of Stanley. If his phone rings, we will know it is him."

Cheryl considered his idea. "You know what? That's not bad. If it's his phone, he has to be the one who placed the ad." She grinned at Levi. "It's brilliant. You really are an ace detective."

Levi snorted. "I have never been described that way before."

"So if we call the number in the advertisement and Stanley answers, then what?" Naomi asked.

Cheryl leaned back in her chair. "Then we must go to Chief Twitchell and tell him everything. After that, there's nothing more we can do. From that point on, it's up to him."

Levi and Naomi considered Cheryl's conclusion and agreed. The three of them discussed a plan based on Levi's idea until they were satisfied with the details.

Cheryl closed the Swiss Miss at five. Then she and Naomi went to the Honey Bee and bought pumpkin spice lattes, sitting outside so they could watch Stanley. Levi had gone to a local feed store to use their public phone. The maze was open until six. At exactly five thirty, Levi was supposed to call the number in the ad. Even though the feed store number would probably show, it was a risk they were willing to take. At least Stanley, aka Jerry, wouldn't suspect them. They hoped he'd just chalk it up to a wrong number. The friends agreed that the most important thing was to see if the number belonged to Stanley.

Cheryl kept looking at her watch, and Naomi just stared at her coffee cup. It was extremely cold outside, but it was the only place the women could think of where they could watch Stanley without arousing too much suspicion. It was almost five thirty when Stanley got up and walked around a corner of the maze, cutting of the women's view of him.

"Sugar and grits!" Cheryl said. "If he doesn't come back, we won't know what's happening."

Naomi reached over and grabbed Cheryl's arm. "Be patient. There is still a little time. We must wait…"

At that very moment, a few seconds past five thirty, Stanley came back into view. The women looked at each other.

He was talking on his phone.

CHAPTER SEVENTEEN

W e've got him," Cheryl said with a sigh of relief. She smiled at Naomi. "I wondered so many times if we were wasting our time, but we actually found him."

Naomi returned the smile, but she wasn't as ebullient as her Englisch friend.

"What's wrong?" Cheryl asked. "I thought you'd be happier than this."

"I am pleased," Naomi said softly, "but I am still concerned for Abby. Even though we found Jerry, I am concerned the chief will not be able to stop him. For good. I pray we have not just made things worse."

Cheryl's excitement over locating Jerry waned some. Was Naomi right? Had they accomplished so little?

"Look, we aren't professional detectives. We've done all we can. Now we need to turn this over to people who know what they're doing. Chief Twitchell seems to be a good man. Janie trusts him. At least let's get his advice. I don't think he'll do anything to put Abby in any further danger." Even as she said the words, she wondered if she were right. Janie's assurances certainly helped some. "We don't really have any other choice," Cheryl said gently. "Unless we catch him committing some kind of crime…"

The women were silent for a while as they finished their lattes. Cheryl had told Naomi the truth. She was out of ideas. Tomorrow was Saturday, and she'd promised Seth their meddling would come to an end.

"So will you talk to the chief tomorrow?" Naomi asked as if she were reading Cheryl's mind.

"Yes." Frankly, Cheryl had planned to go by the station tonight. She was ready to be done with their investigation. But Beau was in his crate in the backseat and was probably ready to get out. Besides, maybe one more night would give her a little more time to come up with an idea that would give them something even more concrete for the chief.

Levi's buggy came down the street and stopped in front of the café. He got out and hurried up the steps.

"Did it work?" he asked as he sat down at their table.

The women nodded. "We saw him on his phone."

"So we caught him? We found Jerry?" Levi looked back and forth between Cheryl and Naomi. "Why do you both look so depressed? I thought you would be more excited."

"We're just not sure we have enough evidence to make a difference," Cheryl said. "Everything we've done may not keep Abby out of danger."

Levi frowned. "I know. But we have done all we can, Cheryl," he said gently. "Now it is time to give what we have learned to someone who can really help Abby."

"I told Janie we'd let them know before we go to the chief," Cheryl said. "I think it's the right thing to do."

"I am in agreement with that," Naomi said. "We must remember that this battle is hers. I will stop by Rachel's house on the way home and speak to her. Then tomorrow, unless she tells us not to, we can go to the police. We need to let her decide what to do next."

"But Stanley...or Jerry, saw you with me, Naomi. Maybe it's not a good idea."

"You mean in case he follows me?"

Cheryl nodded.

"I will keep an eye on him," Levi said. "If I spot him watching us, we will go straight home. Would that set your mind at ease?"

Cheryl nodded. "Yes, it would. Thank you, Levi. Just be very careful."

"I will. I do not take chances with my maam. My daed would have my hide."

Cheryl smiled. "I believe you."

Naomi reached over and patted Cheryl's arm. "Do not worry, my friend. This is a matter for the Lord now," she said. "We need to remember that He is our Protector. If we believe we are the only people who can help Abby, we have done her a disservice. And ignored Gott."

Cheryl smiled at her. "Thank you, Naomi. You're right, of course." She swung her attention to Levi. "Not to change the subject," Cheryl said, "but what did you say to Jerry? I thought you'd just hang up."

"Say to him?" Levi asked. "I do not understand."

Cheryl was confused. "I mean, we saw him talking to you. What did you say?"

Now it was Levi's turn to look perplexed. "I did not talk to him. When his voice mail came on, I hung up."

For a few seconds, Cheryl wondered if Levi didn't understand how a phone worked since a lot of Amish people didn't have them in their homes. But she quickly realized that this didn't make any sense. Levi knew how to use a phone. They used phones for their tourist attractions.

"Wait a minute," she said. "You didn't talk to him?"

Levi shook his head.

Cheryl's mouth dropped open, and Naomi gasped.

"Didn't you see him talking on his phone?" Cheryl asked her.

"Ja," she said. "When he came around the corner of the maze, he was speaking to someone. I am certain."

"Then that means..."

Cheryl stopped midway through her sentence when a police car pulled up in front of the Honey Bee. Chief Twitchell got out and walked up the steps, stopping in front of their table. He didn't look happy.

"I need you all to come down to the station. Right now."

The tone of his voice stopped Cheryl short.

"Is something wrong, Chief?"

Twitchell scowled at them. "Yes, it is."

Cheryl stood up. "I don't understand..."

"Station. Now."

For a moment, Cheryl felt defensive, but she reminded herself she hadn't done anything wrong. Why was the chief upset? She headed to her car, and Naomi and Levi got into their buggy. Although it only took a few minutes to get to the police station, Cheryl felt badly for Beau who seemed to be rather agitated in his crate.

"Just a bit longer," she told him as she got out of the car. She suddenly remembered that she had some treats in the tote bag she used for Beau's things. She reached in and pulled his snack bag out. Immediately, he began to purr. Cheryl pushed several treats through the bars of his crate.

"There, that should keep you until I get back." She got out of the car and waited for Naomi and Levi to arrive. Once they pulled up, the three friends walked toward the station's entrance.

"What is this about?" Levi asked. "Have we broken the law in some way?"

"Of course not," Cheryl said. "We'd know if we had...wouldn't we?" She was trying to sound confident, but in truth, she was a little shaken by the chief's attitude. She'd never been in trouble with the law, but yet, for some reason, she felt a little guilty. It was silly.

They pushed the front door open and went inside. Delores looked up from her desk. She seemed a little surprised to see two Amish people standing in her lobby.

"Well, hello," she said. "What can I do for you?"

"Chief Twitchell told us to come," Cheryl said. She hadn't looked behind her as they drove to the station, but she'd assumed he was following them. She glanced out the window, but the chief's car wasn't there.

"Just a minute." Delores picked up her phone and punched in some numbers. Then she waited. Finally, she put the receiver down. "Well, he doesn't seem to be here yet. Why don't you have a seat?"

Cheryl and Naomi sat down next to each other while Levi stood near them, just staring at the floor. Cheryl was certain this was a new experience for her Amish friends. Maybe that's why she felt a little guilty. Had her involvement in Abby's situation caused this? Just then, Delores's phone rang.

"Okay, gotcha," Delores said. She put the phone down and smiled at them. "The chief came in the back door. You can go on in."

Naomi and Levi followed Cheryl through the frosted door and to the chief's office. Chief Twitchell was sitting behind his desk and motioned for the trio to enter.

"We're a little confused, Chief," Cheryl said as they came inside. "Can you tell us what this is about?"

The chief motioned to some chairs in front of his desk. Naomi and Cheryl sat down while Levi stood behind them.

"Can I ask why you keep botherin' Stanley Gleason?" the chief said sharply.

Cheryl's mouth dropped open. "What? Is that what he told you?"

The chief grunted. "Never mind what he told me. Why are you askin' him questions? Watchin' him?"

Cheryl studied Sam Twitchell for a moment. Just a few minutes earlier she was ready to tell him that Stanley Gleason was really Jerry Harper, but after what Levi told her about the phone call, she wasn't sure about that anymore. All she had were a lot of unproven suspicions. Would the chief think they were just three busybodies who couldn't mind their own business?

"Look," she said finally, "it's true. W…we thought Stanley Gleason was someone else. A man who is looking for his wife.

A wife he's been abusing. But now..." She glanced over at Naomi who looked a little terrified by the prospect of being hauled into a police station.

"And just who is this man? Who did you think Stanley was?"

Cheryl turned to Naomi. "What should we do?"

"I still think we must speak to... Well, you know, before we..."

"I would suggest you ladies tell me everything. Right now," the chief barked. As if realizing his tone was a little harsh, he took a deep breath. "Look, you can talk to me off the record. Just tell me what's going on. Unless someone's broken the law, it will just be between us."

Cheryl hesitated a moment. Then Naomi touched her arm.

"I think we need help," she said softly. "I believe it is time to share our burden."

Trying to start at the beginning, Cheryl began to tell Chief Twitchell the entire story. He stopped her several times to ask questions. Finally she reached the part about Stanley.

"That's the reason we've been watching Stanley. I asked him some questions because I was trying to figure out if he could be Jerry Harper. I guess I was too obvious."

The chief frowned at her. "And do you still think he's this Harper guy?"

"Well, I was fairly confident until..."

"Until what?"

She quickly explained the plan they'd cooked up with the phones. By the time she finished, the chief seemed amused by her story.

"So when Levi said he got Stanley's voice mail, I realized Stanley might not be Jerry after all," Cheryl explained.

Chief Twitchell shook his head. "I must say, you all are very ingenious. You've actually done a remarkable job. Unfortunately, you almost caused a major problem through your misguided attempt to find this Jerry Harper."

Although Cheryl had told the chief almost everything, she'd left out the story about Howard Knisley and the attempt to see his tattoo. Had she mentioned that, she doubted the chief would be quite so complimentary.

"But it seems we haven't helped Abby at all. For all our efforts we've got...nothing."

"Chief, what kind of major problem did we almost cause?" Levi asked.

"First of all, Cheryl," the chief said, "you have more than 'nothin'.' You've got me. We'll figure this out together. And as far as your question, Mr. Miller, can I trust the three of you to keep a secret?"

"Yes, of course," Cheryl said.

Although Levi and Naomi didn't comment, they both nodded.

Chief Twitchell picked up his phone. "Send him in," he said.

They waited in silence until the door to the chief's office opened and a man stepped inside.

Cheryl couldn't hold back a gasp. It was Stanley Gleason.

CHAPTER EIGHTEEN

Good evening," he said. Although the greeting was said without animosity, it was obvious by his expression that Stanley was upset.

"Oh my," Naomi said softly.

Cheryl looked to Chief Twitchell for an explanation.

He seemed amused by their reaction. "Close the door, Stanley."

Stanley pulled the door shut and went over to stand next to the chief who swung his chair around to confront him. "Seems we have a little problem here," he said, addressing the man whom Cheryl thought was Jerry Harper until a little while ago. "These people have been trying to find a man who's been abusin' his wife. They think he's hidin' out in Sugarcreek. In fact, they'd decided you were the man until their plan to catch you backfired on 'em."

Stanley's eyebrows shot up. "Oh, really?" Although he still seemed a little perturbed, Cheryl could see him relax a bit.

"Chief Twitchell, who is this man?" Cheryl asked.

"This is the part I told you about," the chief said. "The thing you need to keep to yourself."

"Wait a minute," Stanley said. "You're not authorized to share this information..."

"Settle down, son," the chief said. "If we don't do a little explainin' to these folks, we risk being exposed by them. They're too smart for us."

"I don't have any idea what you're talking about," Cheryl said, feeling extremely confused. "What's going on?"

The chief stood up. "Ladies and gentleman, I'd like to introduce Martin Shaw. He's with the FBI. He's workin' undercover in Sugarcreek. We've got someone trying to pass funny money around town. Martin is here to catch 'em."

Cheryl's mouth hung open in surprise. "Funny money? FBI?"

The chief nodded. "And his investigation has been producin' some good results. That is until you started pokin' around, askin' questions, and drawin' attention to him."

"W...we thought you were an abusive husband trying to find your wife," Cheryl said.

Martin shook his head. "I assure you, my wife and I get along fine. She's waiting at home for me in Columbus."

Levi cleared his throat. "We did not mean to cause you problems. I hope you will forgive us."

The agent smiled. "I tried not to worry when you started asking me questions. I mean, usually an Amish person isn't a big concern, but when you visited me, Miss Cooper, things became a little worrisome. I couldn't allow you to blow my cover."

"Then when you told me about your friend, Abby," the chief said, "I knew the only thing we could do was just tell you the truth."

"What about this...funny money?" Cheryl asked, concerned for her aunt's store. "Do I have any of it?"

"I don't think so," Martin said, "but it wouldn't hurt for you to go through your cash. If anything looks wrong, let me know. I can check it."

Cheryl nodded. "So the Gleasons are helping you?"

"Yes. Some of the money was passed through their business. They're working with us to find out where it's coming from. We're pretty sure we have the people behind it. A group of counterfeiters are renting a place outside of town, and they're washing some of their fake money through Sugarcreek before they move on. I'm pretty sure we got to them before they did too much damage. We intend to make some arrests on Monday. I just need you three to leave me alone until that happens. You're drawing too much attention to me."

"We won't bother you again," Cheryl said. "I'm so embarrassed."

"Don't be. If we weren't already close to shutting down our investigation, I'd consider hiring you. You three make a good team."

Cheryl knew he was teasing her, but it made her smile. "You're very kind. I'm glad you're not Jerry Harper. But this means..."

"We have failed," Naomi said with a sigh. "We did not find Mr. Harper, and we have not helped Abby at all."

Cheryl patted her friend's arm. "We tried, Naomi. It's all we could do."

"I'll try to help you," Chief Twitchell said, "but from here on out, you need to keep me in the loop."

"Thanks, Chief," Cheryl said. "For now, do you need anything more from us? I have a rather grumpy cat that needs to get home."

The chief stood up. "That's all. Just stay away from Mr. Shaw, please. And maybe it's time to quit lookin' for this Harper character. He's probably long gone by now."

"Maybe you're right. Thanks." Cheryl stood up and walked out the door with Levi and Naomi following her. After saying good-bye to Delores, they walked out of the station and into a town cloaked in dusk. The sun was beginning to set earlier as winter crept toward Sugarcreek. Tonight the moon played peekaboo behind quickly moving clouds. Even at night, Sugarcreek was lovely. Streetlights sparkled, and a cold wind swept colorful leaves through the street. Even though she was disappointed that they hadn't found Jerry, once again, Cheryl felt a rush of gratitude that she was here—and not in her lonely apartment in Columbus. She walked over to Naomi's and Levi's buggy and stroked Sugar's soft face.

"I feel a little foolish," Levi said. "Our amateurish efforts have not produced anything helpful for Abby."

"Ach, Levi," Naomi said soothingly. "Our hearts were right. I do not regret the time we invested. I simply regret that we have not been able to bring the answers Abby seeks." She sighed. "It is late now, and your daed will be wondering about us. I will visit with Rachel tomorrow and let her know that we have not been able to find Jerry. We will pray that Gott will do what we could not."

Cheryl managed to smile at her friends. "Maybe we didn't achieve our goal, but I loved spending time with you both."

Naomi grinned at her. "I am afraid our efforts have caused Mr. Knisley a lifelong fear of coffee."

Cheryl couldn't help but laugh, and Levi joined in.

"Now that is an image I will never forget," he said.

"I'll miss our time together," Cheryl said.

Naomi grabbed her arm. "Ach, Cheryl. Do not be foolish. We are friends. You will probably get tired of us, and tell us to go away." She smiled. "Will you come to supper next Monday night? We would love to have you visit us again."

Cheryl smiled back at her. "Thank you. I would love that."

Naomi gave Cheryl a hug. "Now we had all better get home. The evening air chills my bones."

Cheryl noticed the odd look on Levi's face. "Is something wrong, Levi?" she asked.

He shook his head slowly. "I continue to have the strangest feeling that there is something I have...forgotten."

Cheryl frowned at him. "That's weird. I've been having the same feeling. It's probably because we never found the answers we were looking for."

Naomi made a clucking noise with her tongue. "None of us will have feeling anywhere if we do not get out of the cold." She patted Cheryl's arm. "Go home, my friend. I have some pumpkin bread to bring you tomorrow. I will see you in the morning."

"Thanks. See you then."

"Good night, Cheryl," Levi said in a low voice. "I will be glad to see you at supper next week." He turned quickly away, helping his mother into the buggy then climbing in himself.

Cheryl stood and watched them ride down the street. Then she got inside her car. A quick glance at Beau confirmed her fear that he was getting antsy.

"I'm sorry," she said gently. "I'll make it up with extra kitty treats tonight." As she drove down the street, she kept trying to figure out what it was that kept nagging at her. As far as she could tell, they'd left no stone unturned. Had she missed something? Although she'd never gotten a glimpse of anyone's upper right arm, did it really matter? Stanley wasn't Jerry, and their other two suspects had families. The only conclusion she could draw was that they'd missed Jerry completely. She felt rather silly to think the three of them could have found him anyway. After all, they weren't really detectives. She worked in a shop, and Levi and Naomi were Amish farmers. Why had she ever imagined they could help Abby?

As she drove down Main Street, she noticed a man standing in front of Amazin' Corn. It was the same man who had watched her the other night. Dark poncho and a hat that was pulled down over most of his face. She'd been so sure it was Jerry Harper, but now she knew it was Martin Shaw. She honked her horn and waved at him, but he didn't respond. She immediately chastised herself for her actions. She was supposed to be ignoring him.

"You need to stop it, Cheryl," she said to herself. She checked her rearview mirror, and although Martin didn't respond to her greeting, he watched her as she pulled up in front of the Honey Bee. Beau meowed from the back.

"I'm just getting baked pumpkin holes," she said. "It will only take a minute." She hurried up the steps and only had to wait a minute before being handed a package of the wonderful baked goodies. Shaped like doughnut holes, they were crammed with rich pumpkin flavor and covered with sugar and cinnamon. Cheryl consoled herself with the knowledge that they were baked and not fried. She realized a salad would be a better choice, but tonight she wanted comfort food.

Cheryl looked around for the boy who'd delivered her cookies, but thankfully she didn't see him. He probably thought she was nuts. She wondered if he'd told anyone else about the way she'd acted, but thankfully no one at the café seemed to be looking at her strangely. She put her purse on the counter and reached inside to get her wallet. Once again, the clasp had failed, and her money had spilled out into the purse. She dug through everything until she pulled out the cash she needed, but the gal working the register had to wait on her, as did the people standing in line behind her. She felt certain they were frustrated with how long it took her to find her money.

"Funny running into you here," a voice said.

Cheryl turned around and almost dropped her treat. Martin Shaw stood behind her in the line, and he wasn't wearing a poncho or a hat.

"I . . . I guess it is," she said, looking around. "Weren't you just standing across the street?"

He shook his head. "Not me. Just got here. Picking up some dinner. Bob and Tillie are out of town for the weekend."

Not wanting to draw attention to him, Cheryl just nodded, said good-bye, and hurried out of the café. When she reached her car, she looked back toward the maze, but no one was there. As she drove home, she tried to shake the feeling that something was very, very wrong.

Chapter Nineteen

When she woke up Saturday morning, Cheryl felt better. Convinced she was probably seeing everything through overly suspicious eyes, she tried to shake off the odd foreboding she'd sensed the night before. The man in the poncho could be anyone. He probably wasn't watching her at all. In all likelihood, he was just someone trying to decide if he wanted to go to the Honey Bee for supper. She remembered that Janie had said she'd seen a similar man, but in the light of day, Cheryl realized seeing someone in a rain poncho during the past few days was absolutely normal. Almost everyone had donned their rain gear during the recent downpours.

After loading Beau up in the car, she drove to work trying not to think about the meeting that would take place today between Naomi and Abby. She felt badly that they hadn't been able to help her.

When she pulled up to the Swiss Miss, she was surprised to see Ben Vogel sitting on a bench on the porch. The Vogel brothers usually came in later, after the doors opened.

She got Beau's crate out of the car and hurried up the steps. "Good morning," she said, not expecting much of a response.

"Good morning," he said softly. "I wonder if I might speak to you for a moment before your day begins."

Cheryl was surprised by his request. This was the first time he'd ever really spoken an entire sentence to her. She smiled. "Of course. Please come in." She unlocked the door and held it open. "I hope you haven't been waiting long."

He shook his head and followed her up toward the counter. First Cheryl took the crate into her office and let Beau out. Listening to him yowl while trying to talk to Ben was something she wanted to avoid. The persnickety feline would want his breakfast soon, but he would probably give them a few minutes before insisting she feed him. Beau ran straight for Ben and rubbed up against his pant leg. Ben leaned over to pet him, a smile on his face. Cheryl noticed he was holding an old cloth bag, and she wondered what was in it.

"I have a confession," he said when he straightened. "Hopefully, you will be able to accept my apology for a rather devious plot on my part."

Cheryl frowned at him. "I'm sorry, Ben. I don't understand." The elderly man pulled the bag open and emptied it on the counter. Cheryl gasped when she saw an Amish doll, a carved wooden horse, and several lovely embroidered dish towels. "The things on my shelves. It...it was you?"

He nodded. "You see, my brother Rueben has a grandchild, Betsy. She made all these items. She is very talented, but also quite shy. I offered to talk to you about putting them in your store, but she was too nervous. So I began placing them on your shelves so I could prove to her that people would like her work. I hope I didn't cause you too much trouble. It wasn't my intention."

"No, it wasn't a lot of trouble," Cheryl said. "I was just curious about it. I love everything Betsy has made, and I would be honored to carry them in the store. Will you ask her to come by and talk to me?"

Ben smiled. Something she'd never seen him do before. A movement behind Ben made her glance toward the front door. Thankfully, the bell didn't ring because the door was opened so slowly. Quickly redirecting her attention back to Ben, she frowned at the elderly man. "I must admit that I'm a little confused about something. I mean…if your brother sees you as…"

"Shunned?" Ben finished for her. "Why am I talking to my great-niece?"

Cheryl nodded.

"Because Betsy is a sweet, lovely child. Even though I tried to discourage her, she reached out to me. Wouldn't leave me alone until I would talk to her. Over the last couple of years we have become…close." He shook his head. "It wasn't my intention, and I'm afraid my brother might be very upset with me if he finds out that we have developed a relationship. I have caused him enough grief, and the last thing I want to do is to upset him any further. I cherish our games together. It's all I have left of my brother, and I don't want to lose it. He is very important to me. And so is Betsy. I love her very much, and I felt compelled to help her."

"So you don't think Rueben will appreciate what you've done?"

"Sadly, no. I would do anything to mend the past, but I cannot go back to the Amish church. To do so would be dishonest. I am glad he has found happiness in the church. I would never ask him to leave. I accept his choices. If only he would accept mine and still welcome me as his brother." He sighed deeply. "But I am afraid my brother will never understand this."

Cheryl took a deep breath. "Maybe you're wrong," she said softly. "Why don't you ask him?"

Ben looked confused. When someone cleared his throat behind him, he turned around to see Rueben standing just inside the door. Cheryl held her breath and prayed silently—but fervently. For several seconds, the two brothers just stared at each other. Finally, Rueben headed toward the checkers table.

Tears sprung to Cheryl's eyes when she heard him say, "It is a little early for our game, Brother, but I have some extra time today. Perhaps we can get an additional match in."

Ben turned back to Cheryl, his own eyes wet with emotion. He pushed the items on the counter toward her. "I will ask Betsy to come by and see you. Thank you so much for your kindness."

Cheryl nodded, not trusting herself to respond. Ben turned and shuffled toward the checkerboard, sat down, and waited until his brother made the first move. Beau, who seemed to have forgotten his breakfast, ran over and curled up under the table, one paw on Ben's shoe.

Cheryl hurried to the back office, carrying Betsy's new craft items with her. She grabbed a tissue from the bathroom, cried a bit, wiped her eyes, and then went back out into the shop. Yesterday had been rather depressing, but this morning she'd witnessed a miracle. She could hardly wait to write Mitzi and tell her what had happened. Her aunt would be overjoyed.

The morning passed quickly with tourists flooding into town. Cheryl was grateful for Lydia's help. She worked Saturday mornings, and Esther worked the afternoon. If things were incredibly busy, Lydia would also stay for a while after lunch. Mitzi had warned Cheryl that during late fall and winter, business would fall off. At that point, Cheryl could switch to winter hours, but so far, the shop was too busy for her to even consider it.

Once again, the bus from Annie's Amish Tours pulled up across the street, but Howard stayed on the bus. At some point, Cheryl knew she would have to try to talk to him a second time. Apologize for her actions. Maybe she would simply tell him the truth. Perhaps understanding what they were trying to do for Abby would help him to forgive her.

Around eleven thirty, Lydia left. A little before noon, Esther walked in, Naomi and Levi on her heels. Levi was holding a large plastic container.

Cheryl smiled at Naomi. "I forgot you were coming today." she said.

"We decided to bring you a treat," Levi said. "After yesterday, we assumed you could use one, ain't so?"

Cheryl grinned. "Very much so. Besides, I have something to tell you."

"Is it about Jerry?" Naomi asked.

Cheryl shook her head. "Sadly, no. But something wonderful happened here this morning. You'll be very happy to hear about it."

"We could use some good news," Levi said. "I look forward to your exciting story."

Cheryl nodded. The brothers were gone now, but their game had lasted twice as long as usual, and even though there wasn't a lot of discussion, Cheryl had heard them speak briefly to each other. When they left, Rueben held the door open for his brother. Cheryl's joy at their reconciliation helped to balance her disappointment in not finding Jerry Harper. Last night she'd run everything over in her mind several times, trying to figure out if there was something she'd missed. All she ended up with was the same odd feeling that Levi had expressed. Something that kept nagging at her. Try as she might, she hadn't been able to figure out what it was.

After telling Esther they would be in her office, Cheryl opened the door and led her friends inside. Naomi put the container of brownies on Cheryl's desk. There were still some paper plates and napkins from their picnic lunch, so Cheryl fetched them from a nearby cabinet. A few minutes later, they were munching on brownies and coffee. Beau, who'd had his breakfast after the brothers left, sauntered in, acting cool.

"Don't let him fool you," Cheryl said with a grin. "He's looking for a handout."

Naomi chuckled. "I did not forget my friend. I brought him something from home." She reached into her pocket and took out a piece of chicken. Naomi tore off a small bit and offered it to the friendly Siamese. His tail went straight up with pleasure, and he quickly snatched the chicken before Naomi could change her mind.

"So you said you had something to tell us?" Levi asked.

As Cheryl recounted her meeting with Ben and the subsequent scene between Rueben and his brother, Naomi's and Levi's smiles grew wide.

"Ach, this is wonderful news," Naomi said. "I have been praying for a long time."

"So you don't believe in shunning either?" Cheryl asked.

Naomi paused a moment before answering. "I was brought up under this teaching. I know it sounds cruel to you, but you must understand that the reason for this measure was to save those who might wander away from the church. It was done out of love for them, even though it caused families much pain. Our local church only shuns if someone is involved in sin and is unrepentant. For example, a couple of years ago, a certain man was caught cheating on his wife. He was counseled by our bishop and by the elders. After repenting to them and to his wife, he lived differently for a while, but eventually he went back to his previous lifestyle. At that time, the elders removed him from the church, but only after trying one more time to reconcile him. He refused. However, if the day comes that he truly repents and wants to return, the church would receive him."

Cheryl shrugged. "Actually, I think that's the way most churches handle that kind of thing."

"That may be right, I do not know. As far as the Vogel brothers, more than once our bishop spoke to Rueben, encouraging him to heal old wounds, but Rueben was unable to accept his counsel. I think he felt he would be turning his back on the faith his parents taught him."

"But a little child will lead them," Cheryl said.

Levi nodded. "Betsy is a sweet girl, and I know she will be thrilled to find out what her efforts have achieved."

"And now you have solved the problem of the unusual items showing up in your store," Naomi said with a smile. "At least that is one mystery solved, ain't so?"

Cheryl nodded. "Yes, but I sure wish we'd solved our other mystery. The whereabouts of Jerry Harper."

"Ach, I do too," Naomi said. "But we must move past it. I am praying for Abby. Gott does not need our help protecting His children."

Cheryl nodded. "I know that's true. I guess I kind of forget sometimes."

"It is because you wanted so much to help her," Levi said, his dark blue eyes focused on Cheryl. "It is because you have a kind heart."

Cheryl smiled. "Thanks. Unfortunately, my heart didn't do Abby much good." She frowned at Naomi. "I'll go with you to speak to Abby. You shouldn't have to do it alone."

Naomi shook her head. "I do not think this is wise. What if Jerry really is in town somewhere, Cheryl? I believe a visit from me would be less suspicious than one from you, ja?"

Cheryl thought over Naomi's reasoning. Once again, a picture of the man in the poncho flashed in her head. Even though she had convinced herself he had nothing to do with their search for Jerry, maybe exercising caution would be prudent.

"I appreciate it, Naomi," she said. "When will you go?"

"I have some deliveries to make this afternoon. I will probably stop by on the way home this evening."

Cheryl nodded. "After I close the store, I'm going to Buttons 'n' Bows. I've got to have a new wallet. If you see my car outside the shop on your way home, will you stop and let me know how it went?"

"Yes, I will certainly do so," Naomi said.

"I assume you told Seth about our meeting with Chief Twitchell?" Cheryl blurted out. She was certain they had, but she wanted to make sure her friendship with Naomi was still intact. She'd been worried about it ever since she spoke to Seth at their house.

"Yes," Levi said after swallowing the last of his brownie. "He is also sorry we were not able to find Jerry." He smiled at her. "But he is glad Maam has found such a wonderful friend. There is nothing to be concerned about."

Cheryl breathed a deep sigh of relief.

The door to the office swung open, and Esther came in. "Lydia is here," she said. "Would it be all right if I left around two o'clock? If we are not busy."

"You've worked extra hours this week," Cheryl said. "That would be fine."

"Thank you, Cheryl," Esther said. She noticed the large container of brownies on Cheryl's desk. She grinned at her mother. "Lydia and I would be willing to help you with those brownies."

Naomi laughed. "I am sure you would. You may both have a brownie."

Esther turned and called out to Lydia. When the girl came into the office, Cheryl was shocked to see her. She had changed clothes since the morning, and her hair was different. A large streak of purple hair had been pinned into her own dark hair. Her makeup was heavier, with dark eyeliner circling her eyes. Her simple dress had been replaced with tight jeans and a black T-shirt that sported a bright pink symbol. Cheryl recognized it as the logo of a heavy metal band. Not a band Cheryl was familiar with, but she'd heard about it.

Naomi gasped and jumped to her feet. "Esther, you will not go out with Lydia today. Not when she looks like...this. I forbid it."

CHAPTER TWENTY

There was silence as Esther stared back at her mother. Finally, she averted her eyes. "Yes, Maam." She closed the door quietly without getting a brownie.

Naomi looked over at Levi who seemed to be concentrating on his food. "Do you think I am wrong, Son?" she asked. "Lydia's apparel is...beyond inappropriate, ain't so?"

He finished chewing while Naomi sat down again. "Maam, it is not my job to parent Esther. As you know, I did not engage in rumspringa, but I do understand the purpose behind it. Do you want Esther to be baptized because it is your wish? Or because it is hers?"

Naomi straightened her back, and her face flushed with emotion. "I want it to be her decision, but there are some things I will not allow. I realize not all parents agree with me, but I will not stand by and watch my children act unseemly just because...they can. If this makes me a poor mother, I do not care. So be it."

Frankly, Cheryl agreed with Naomi, but she kept her opinion to herself.

"I do not think being seen with Lydia in her worldly clothes is...unseemly," Levi said gently. "Esther has not chosen to dress that way—or to participate in any of the things you mentioned. She is a good girl."

"I know she is a good girl," Naomi huffed. "I did not say she was anything else."

"Do you think she will follow Lydia in these attempts to get attention?"

Naomi frowned at her son. "What do you mean?"

Levi sighed. "Lydia is one of nine children, ain't so?"

Naomi nodded.

"It occurs to me that she and her brother, Thomas, are the only ones engaged in rumspringa," Levi said. "But Thomas is not interested in anything except working their farm. Now all the attention is on Lydia, something that has never happened before."

"Well, perhaps the girl should seek attention by doing good," Naomi snapped back. "Not by trying to lead your sister astray."

Levi smiled at his mother. "I understand, Maam. Perhaps it was hearing Cheryl tell us about Ben and Rueben, but maybe offering understanding to Lydia would do more good than our anger. Esther will be fine. Lydia does not have the power to change who you have taught her to be. 'Mothers write on the hearts of their children what the world's rough hand cannot erase.' You have told us this many times, ja?"

Naomi was silent as she drank her coffee. She didn't forget to offer another tidbit to Beau who now sat at her feet. "I suppose I have been in fear," she said finally. "I do not want to lose Esther to the world."

"Then trust her," Levi said. "And trust the seed you have sown into her life. Let her know you support her. Esther is not Lydia . . . or Sarah. She will not leave you, Maam. If you search your heart, is this not what you truly believe?"

Naomi glanced at Cheryl, who smiled at her friend. Although she kept quiet during their discussion, Cheryl agreed with Levi. She'd also wondered if Lydia were using rumspringa as a means to get attention. But Esther had a good heart. In the end, Cheryl believed she would make the best decision for her, no matter what Lydia said or did.

"Yes, this is what I believe," Naomi said with a sigh. "And perhaps a little positive attention shown to Lydia would do more to draw her to faith than a negative reaction."

Levi shrugged. "Whatever you decide," he said nonchalantly. He ate one last brownie in two bites and stood up. "I must get back to the farm. I will get your cart out of the buggy, Maam. Are you certain you do not need me to carry you around today?"

Naomi shook her head and began to gather up the paper plates and napkins. "I am only going to businesses on Main Street. My cart will work just fine." She pointed at the container of brownies. "Keep these here," she said to Cheryl. "For you and...your helpers."

Cheryl realized she felt badly that Esther and Lydia hadn't had brownies. "I'll make sure they're eaten," she said with a smile. "No worries there."

"Thank you, Cheryl," Levi said. "I realize eating Maam's brownies is an act of sacrifice. I suffer every day, forcing myself to choke down her cooking."

Naomi snorted and slapped her son lightly on the arm. "See what I must endure from this boy?" she said to Cheryl.

Cheryl laughed at them. This was obviously their way of patching over disagreements. The love in the Miller family touched her. She was close to her parents, but not as close to her brother, Matt. The Millers had something very special. Suddenly, Cheryl longed to see her mother and father. Maybe she should extend an invitation to visit Sugarcreek. It had been almost a year since the three of them had been together.

"So you have a cart?" Cheryl asked Naomi, turning her attention back to the business at hand. She'd never seen her do deliveries without Levi.

"Yes. I must have help from one of my boys for large deliveries, but with smaller items my cart works very well. Seth made it for me. I just push it down the sidewalks. It is light and easy to maneuver. Seth is very good at creating whatever we need to accomplish our work."

Cheryl followed them out and into the shop. Esther was standing behind the counter, and Lydia was near the door. When she saw Naomi, she put her hand on the doorknob, preparing to leave.

"Lydia, you did not have a brownie, ain't so?" Naomi said. She pointed at Esther. "You girls go back into the office and help yourself, ja? They are very good brownies, even if I do say so myself."

Esther's eyes widened at her mother's statement, and although Lydia took her hand off the doorknob, she still looked unsure.

Naomi walked over to Lydia and put her hand on the girl's shoulder. "I am sorry, Lydia. I am concerned about some of the choices you are making, but you have always been a good girl. A good friend to Esther. I must trust that you will not try to influence her in ways that would not make her happy. I may not always agree with you, but I love you, and I will pray for you."

Lydia's eyes filled with tears. "Thank you," she whispered.

"You are welcome. Now get a brownie, and then you girls go on and spend the afternoon having fun." She turned back to Esther. "Your brother will pick us up around five o'clock, Esther. We will meet out front, ja?"

"Ja, Maam," Esther said with a smile. "I will be there."

The girls hurried into the office as Levi walked over and wrapped his arms around his mother. "Mothers are a gift from Gott," he said before saying good-bye to Cheryl and going outside to the buggy.

Cheryl watched through the front window as he took out a small wooden cart with wheels and a long handle from a back storage area in the buggy. The cart was built like a sturdy wagon, but it was square and very deep. The wheels were light and rather large, which would probably make it easy for Naomi to push. The wood had been painted a light blue with colorful flowers around the edges of each side. In the middle the words *Millers' Farm* had been stenciled.

Naomi and Cheryl went outside on the front porch to watch him. "I love your cart," Cheryl said as Levi began to load it up with jars of jam, jelly, cheese, baked goods, and other things.

"Ja, it is a blessing." She nodded toward Levi, who was putting items inside the cart. "Is there anything you need today?"

"No, I'm good," Cheryl said. "But I'm making a list of several items for next week."

Naomi nodded. "Maybe you can bring the list Monday night. That way we can make a delivery on Tuesday?"

"Sounds good."

Esther and Lydia came out on the porch, getting ready to take off. But before she left, Lydia stopped and came back to Naomi.

"Thank you," she said again. "You shouldn't worry about Esther. She influences me more than I influence her. That's why I value her friendship so much. She is just like you." With that, she turned and followed Esther down the steps and out onto the sidewalk.

"Oh my," Naomi said softly.

Cheryl gave her friend a hug. "Smart girl," she said.

Naomi smiled as she gently pulled herself out of Cheryl's embrace. "You will give me a big head. I must get to work."

Cheryl watched Naomi hurry to her cart, grateful her friendship had survived their failed attempts to help Abby Harper.

Although the rest of the afternoon was rather slow, the time went by quickly. When five o'clock rolled around, Cheryl locked the door, put Beau in his crate, and headed out to her car. She had just put the crate in her backseat when Levi pulled up in the buggy.

"Maam is not back?" he asked.

Cheryl shook her head. "I haven't seen her."

He sighed. "She starts to visit, and the time gets away from her. Hopefully, I will not have to wait long. We have a problem with one of our cows. She is having a hard time feeding her newborn calf. I need to get back to the farm soon."

Cheryl glanced up and down the streets, but she didn't see Naomi anywhere. "I'm headed to Buttons 'n' Bows. If I see her, I'll tell her you're waiting."

"Thank you, Cheryl," he said.

Cheryl got into her car and drove away, watching Levi in her rearview mirror. He really was one of the nicest men she'd ever known. She couldn't help but compare him to Lance. The difference between them was remarkable. Lance's main concern had always been for himself. Cheryl had always felt it was her responsibility to fit into his life—into his plans. But Levi put other people first. He was good and gentle, and Cheryl trusted him.

When she realized she was actually measuring Levi by Lance, she flushed with embarrassment. "Stop that!" she said to herself. "You're not Amish, and you'll never be Amish. Levi is a friend, and that is all he'll ever be." As she considered her words, she realized that maybe it was all right to compare him to other men. After all, as long as she never confused friendship with something else, perhaps there wasn't any harm in admiring attributes she'd like to see in a man she might meet in the future. In fact, it could help her immensely. She realized that if she'd met Levi first, she never would have been attracted to Lance. His selfish attitudes would have been much more obvious.

Satisfied that she didn't need to feel guilty any longer, she began to look forward to her trip to Buttons 'n' Bows. It was a darling shop with purses, wallets, tote bags, belts, and even jewelry. They had just started adding some jackets and sweaters for fall. The owners, Gail Murray and her daughter, Kim, were lovely women who had come by the Swiss Miss several times. Cheryl was happy to finally be doing some business in their store. Thankfully, they stayed open until six, so Cheryl could make it to the shop before they closed.

She pulled up in front and parked. As she got out of the car, she looked up and down the street. Still no Naomi. Although she was certain Levi was right about his mother stopping to talk and forgetting the time, she felt a little twinge of worry. Hopefully, her friend was all right. After buying a wallet, she intended to go back by the office to make sure she'd made it back to meet Levi.

"Good evening," a male voice said.

Cheryl turned around to find Mike Taylor standing on the sidewalk in front of the shop.

"Hello," she said. "Still in town?"

He smiled. "Yes, but I'm headed out soon. Hard to leave, but I've got to get home."

Cheryl stepped up onto the store's porch. "I'm sorry you didn't find what you wanted in Sugarcreek. I hope you won't give up. It's a wonderful town."

He shrugged. "I made some good contacts. One of these days I'll find something. But for now, I guess I'll keep my job and wait."

Cheryl held out her hand. "Well, good luck. When you come back, stop by and say hello."

He smiled and shook her hand. "Thanks, I'll do that. Well, I'd better get going. I'm headed to Yoder's. One last meal there before I leave. My diet has flown out the door since I got here. My wife will have to let out all my pants."

Cheryl laughed. "I know exactly what you mean. I keep telling myself I'll eat less...tomorrow."

Mike grinned. "But tomorrow never comes?"

"Not so far."

He pointed at the store. "Shopping here?"

She sighed. "Yes, my wallet has given up the ghost, I'm afraid. I so admired your wallet, so I thought I'd stop in to see what they have for women."

Mike nodded. "They're pretty expensive here. I saw some nice women's purses and wallets at Maxine's on Fourth Street."

Cheryl knew the store, but many of the items were cheaply made. She could save money, but whatever she bought probably wouldn't last as long.

"I think I'll try here first, but thanks for the tip."

He nodded, said a quick good-bye, and walked away. Cheryl watched him as he headed down the street toward Yoder's. Nice man, but he seemed to suddenly lose interest in their conversation. Cheryl wondered if she'd said something to offend him. Surely he couldn't be upset because she'd ignored his advice about Maxine's. She shrugged. Probably had something else on his mind. When Cheryl was a teenager, she was frequently afraid people were upset with her. Her father had taught her that most of the time when people were abrupt or rude, it had nothing to do with her. It was a simple but valuable lesson that had taught her she wasn't really the center of everyone else's universe. This knowledge had helped her a lot in her dealings with people. Choosing not to overthink Mike's reaction, she opened the door to Buttons 'n' Bows and went inside.

"Why hello, Cheryl!" Gail called out. "Nice to see you."

"It's nice to see you too," Cheryl said with a smile. She pointed to a new display of leather jackets and knitted sweaters. "Gearing up for winter?"

Gail laughed. "And fall. It can get pretty cold around here. Never too early. What can I help you with?"

"My nine-year-old wallet is past redemption," Cheryl said. "The other day I saw a man's wallet you sold, and it was so well made. I'm hoping to find a women's wallet that's just as nice."

"I think we can help you," Gail said. "Our wallets are over here."

Cheryl followed Gail over to a large table. Gail was an attractive middle-aged woman with short silver hair and a bouncy, energetic attitude. Mitzi had told Cheryl that Gail's husband had died several years ago in a traffic accident. Although he'd left his wife with plenty of insurance money, Kim, their daughter, could see her mother becoming more and more reclusive. Kim was the one who'd come up with the idea of opening a shop. Gail had always had a passion for purses, so Buttons 'n' Bows began as just a purse store. Over the last year, they'd started to branch out. Although Kim helped in the store quite a bit, she also had to spend time at home with Gail's brand-new grandson.

"As you can see, we have a really large selection." Gail took off a pair of glasses that had been balanced on her nose. "I don't know why I wear these," she said with exasperation. "It's like looking through plain glass. No help at all." She rubbed her nose. "Plus they pinch." She smiled at Cheryl. "You're lucky not to have to wear glasses."

Cheryl nodded, but her mind was somewhere else. That odd feeling was back. There was something about what Gail said that disturbed her, but she couldn't connect it to anything concrete.

She forced herself to turn her attention back to the wallets. They were absolutely lovely. Some of them were fancy, with rhinestones and designs, and others were much plainer. She saw a deep purple brushed suede wallet with a simple design on the front. Since purple was Cheryl's favorite color, she felt drawn to it and picked it up.

"That's a lovely model," Gail said. "One of my favorites. It should last you a long time."

Cheryl snuck a look at the price tag and was happy to learn it wasn't as expensive as she'd thought it might be. She flipped it open to check out the inside. What she saw caused her to cry out, drop the wallet, and run out of the building.

Cheryl had found Jerry Harper.

CHAPTER TWENTY-ONE

O nce outside, she jumped in her car, wondering just what to do next. "I need to talk to Levi and Naomi," she said to herself. Beau yowled from the backseat, trying to let her know he was ready to go home. "Not yet," she said. "Sorry, but I have something to do first." Remembering that Levi had been at the store and that Naomi was supposed to meet him there, Cheryl drove back to the Swiss Miss, hoping to find them. She realized on the way that she'd made a huge mistake. Her first destination should have been the police station. Since she was already pulling up in front of the store, she decided to go inside and call Chief Twitchell. Cheryl was dismayed to see that the Millers weren't there. They might not have been able to help her, but she would feel better having them near. Not knowing what else to do, she grabbed Beau, ran inside, and hurried back to her office. She had her hand on the phone when she heard the bell over the door jingle. Hoping it might be Levi and Naomi, she put the phone down and went out into the shop. Mike Taylor was just closing the door.

"You certainly headed back here quickly," he said with an odd smile. "Did something happen to upset you?"

Cheryl just stared at him. "You need to leave," she said finally. "I know who you are."

Mike turned slightly, still keeping his eyes on her. Cheryl watched him lock the door.

"I shouldn't have shown you the picture that came with my wallet. I figured if you thought it was my family, it would lower your suspicions. I had no idea you'd get it into your head to buy a wallet at the same store. I guess your wallet was made by the same company that manufactured mine. That was bad luck."

"You've been watching me."

He shrugged. "At first I was only concerned that you'd over-heard me in the corn maze. That's why I sent you that note. I had no idea you knew where my wife was, but when you told me you were looking for someone, I realized you must know about her. And me. At least you had no idea who I was—until now. Your reaction at Buttons 'n' Bows made that crystal clear. Most people wouldn't remember a picture in a wallet. But you did, didn't you?"

Cheryl wondered if she could have explained away her actions at the store. Telling him just now that she knew his true identity had been a huge blunder. But it was too late now. The cat was out of the bag. "I'm not going to tell you anything," she said. "I won't put Abby in danger."

Jerry pulled down the shades on the front window so no one could see inside the store from the front porch. "I'm afraid you won't have much of a choice. I don't want to hurt you, but I will if I have to. Abby is my wife, and I have no intention of allowing her to leave me. We can work out our problems. We just need other people to keep their noses out of our business."

Cheryl's mouth dropped open. "Abby doesn't want to work out your problems. You hit her, Jerry. That's not okay. Ever."

His features tightened, and Cheryl wondered if she was seeing the face Abby had seen before he struck her. She felt herself stiffen with fear, but fought back, trying to stay calm.

"She has a friend who lives here. Janie Henderson. Someone at Abby's reunion told me she and Janie spent quite a bit of time talking the night of the reunion. I was sure Abby was with her, but I've kept a close eye on Janie's place. No Abby. I almost gave up and left, but then you and your Amish friends caught my attention. I decided to stay and keep my eye on you. Obviously, that was the right decision."

"Was that you in the poncho and wearing a hat?"

He nodded. "Obviously, shadowing you finally paid off."

He took off his glasses and put them in his pocket.

"It was the glasses," Cheryl said softly, more to herself than to him.

"Excuse me?"

"Your glasses. Something kept nagging at me. Just plain glass. No magnification. I should have realized they were just part of your disguise."

He shook his head. "Whatever. My disguise accomplished what I needed. I'm tired of looking for my wife. I must say, someone has done a good job of hiding her." He took a couple of steps toward Cheryl. "But now you're going to tell me where she is."

"No, I won't."

He reached into an inside coat pocket. Cheryl gasped when he pulled out a gun.

"I'm not going to fool around with you, Cheryl. Either you tell me what I want to know, or you'll be sorry. It's as simple as that."

Cheryl's mind felt numb. She prayed silently for help. What could she do? How could she get out of this? Before she had a chance to respond, the door behind them swung open. Jerry whirled around to find Chief Twitchell standing there, his gun drawn.

"Put it down," he barked. "Now. I won't ask you a second time."

"Don't shoot," Jerry said quickly. "Please don't shoot." He slowly lowered the weapon to the floor.

"Now back up," the chief said.

Jerry took a couple of steps back. The chief walked over and picked up the gun. He put it on a nearby shelf, and then he took a pair of handcuffs off his belt, and within a couple of minutes Jerry was restrained.

"Ach, Cheryl!" Naomi said as she rushed through the door. "Are you all right?"

Levi was behind her, and they both hurried over to where Cheryl stood, shaking. "I...I think so. Why are you here? And...how did you get in?"

Naomi put her arms around Cheryl. "Come over here and sit down. You are trembling."

Cheryl lowered herself into the rocking chair. Out of the corner of her eye, she saw another police officer escort Jerry out of the shop.

"We were coming up the street when we saw you run out of Buttons 'n' Bows," Naomi said gently. "Levi went inside to find out what had happened. When Gail showed us the wallet, Levi put two and two together. The new wallet. A picture of a woman and two children, but Mike was not in the picture. It was because the picture came with the wallet."

Levi nodded. "Once I began to think about Mike, I realized what had been bothering me so much," Levi said. "Mike said he lived in Loudonville."

"So?" Cheryl said.

"Remember that he claimed he needed to go home so he wouldn't miss Octoberfest?"

Cheryl nodded.

"Loudonville's Octoberfest is actually in September. Not October. It has already been held. Anyone who lived in Loudonville would know that."

"And we got inside because Mitzi gave me a key," Naomi said. "A long time ago. In case of emergencies. I would have given it back to you, but I forgot all about it. Until just now. I actually keep it in a special place in the cart. It is so odd that I would have the cart today—when I needed that key."

Cheryl wiped away a tear that ran down the side of her face. "God used Aunt Mitzi to save the day again. Even though she's not actually here."

Naomi laughed. "My friend Mitzi is funny that way, ja? Showing up or saying something at just the right time."

"Yes, she certainly has great timing."

Chief Twitchell walked up to the trio. "Excuse me," he said, "but I'll need to talk to you, Cheryl. I will actually need to talk to all of you, but I can wait and meet with you two"—he pointed at Naomi and Levi—"sometime tomorrow."

"Sunday?" Naomi said. "I do not think..."

The chief smiled. "Sorry. You're right. Monday will be fine." He turned his attention to Cheryl. "I'll need a brief statement from you now," he said. "Just confirming that this man threatened your life. That he pulled a gun on you."

"I can certainly do that," she said. "How long will you be able to hold him?"

"Chief?"

A second police officer had stepped inside the shop. Cheryl wondered how many officers had responded to the situation. Lights from police cars flashed outside, illuminating the night with reds and blues.

Twitchell turned toward his officer. "What's up, Anderson?"

"I think you need to see this."

"Excuse me a minute," the chief said. "I'll be right back."

Once he walked away, Naomi grabbed Cheryl's hand and knelt down next to her. "I praise Gott that he brought us by the store just in time. The wheel on my cart broke and delayed my deliveries. Levi had to come and find me. The delay was Gott watching over you."

Cheryl tried to blink back the tears that filled her eyes. "I'm very grateful to Him—and to you. If you hadn't come..."

Naomi squeezed her hand. "Gott would have sent someone else, ja? He does not need us. He just needs those who are willing to follow Him."

Cheryl suddenly realized something. "I guess we finally have some good news to share with Abby."

Levi nodded. "As long as Jerry will be put away for a while. If he is let out immediately . . ."

"That won't happen." The chief had come back into the room. "Besides threatening your life, we just discovered that his car was stolen from someone in Nebraska. Seems Jerry beat the car's owner with a bat. He's in the hospital. May be a long time before he recovers. Along with this situation, Jerry's facing grand theft and aggravated assault. He won't see the light of day for a long, long time."

Although Cheryl couldn't help feeling sad to see another human being's life take such an awful turn, she was relieved for Abby. At last, now she would be free to get the help she needed.

"We will pray for him," Naomi said, rising to her feet. "No one is so far away from Gott that they cannot be redeemed."

"Yes," Levi said. "We will keep him in prayer."

Cheryl was feeling a little less spiritual than her friends. She'd never had a gun pointed at her before, but she nodded anyway. "Thank you, Chief, for coming so quickly," she said. "You were just in time."

The chief grinned. "Well, when a young Amish man comes running into the station, breaks into my office, and tells me that his friend is in 'imminent danger,' I have to respond." He shook his head. "I can only hope I have friends who care about me the way these two care about you, young lady."

Cheryl looked back and forth between Naomi and Levi. "I am very blessed," she said softly.

"If you could come down to the station for a little bit," he said to Cheryl, "I could get a quick statement so you can go home. We'll talk more on Monday."

"How long will that take?" Cheryl asked.

The chief shrugged. "Not longer than thirty minutes. I already know quite a bit about the situation." He frowned. "And I will need to talk to Jerry's wife. Can you let her know that?"

"Yes. Do you need to talk to her right now?"

"Well, not this very minute. After you and I talk."

"We can let her know as soon as you're through with me. Would that be okay?"

The chief nodded. "That would be fine."

Cheryl stood up and took Naomi's arm. "I know this is asking a lot, but could you wait until I'm done? I'd love to be there when we tell Abby that Jerry is in jail."

Naomi smiled. "Ach, as if we would visit her without you." She hugged Cheryl. "You go to the station and talk to the chief. Perhaps we can wait here with Beau until you come back? Then we can all go to Rachel's together?" She reached into a pocket in her dress and handed Cheryl a key. "Here. I should return this."

Cheryl put her hands over Naomi's and folded her fingers over the palmed key. "Please, keep it. I feel so much better knowing you have it."

"All right. I will keep it gladly."

"I will drive home and tell Daed why we are running late tonight," Levi said to his mother. He turned to Cheryl. "I will be back before you return." He smiled at her, and Cheryl felt her heart jump.

She followed the chief out of the shop and drove behind him to the station. The car carrying Jerry was gone. Cheryl was relieved. She had no desire to ever see him again.

Once she reached the station, it only took about twenty minutes to finish the report. She told the chief she'd come back Monday afternoon with Naomi and Levi and then left.

When she stepped outside, she took a deep breath. The fall air was crisp and fresh, and someone was burning leaves. The aroma was intoxicating. Cheryl got back in her car and drove slowly back to the shop, gazing at the stores and buildings along the way. On her way, she stopped in front of Buttons 'n' Bows and was delighted to find it still open. She ran in, bought the wallet she'd been looking at, and left. She could only give Gail a brief explanation for her actions since she didn't want anyone else to know about Abby, but Gail didn't seem to be too concerned about it.

"I'm just glad you're okay," she said. "I must say I've never had anyone react like that to our merchandise."

Gail's lighthearted comment made Cheryl laugh. After saying good-bye, she drove the rest of the way to the Swiss Miss. Levi was back. Naomi grinned at her as she came inside.

"Mr. Beau is ready to go home, I think. He has been quite feisty."

Cheryl laughed at the silly cat who hid behind Naomi's skirt, batting at her hem. "Let's get out of here," she said.

It took a while to catch him because he kept trying to run from her, but with Levi's help, Beau was finally loaded back into his crate. Levi and Naomi went outside to their buggy while Cheryl locked up. Then she got in her car and followed them to Rachel's house.

Cheryl smiled all the way there.

CHAPTER TWENTY-TWO

Monday morning was bright but cold. Cheryl got to work a little late. After church Sunday morning, she'd spent the remainder of the day just resting. For some reason, she was exhausted. Probably just a release from the stress of looking for Jerry Harper. Abby had been beside herself with joy Saturday evening. Although she elected to stay in town for a little while longer, she planned to go home and stay with her parents until she could get back on her feet. Cheryl advised her that Chief Twitchell needed to see her on Monday.

"No problem," she'd said with a smile. "In fact, I'd like to get out and see some of this wonderful town." She'd hugged Cheryl and Naomi with enthusiasm. "I will never be able to thank you enough for what you've done. Without you, Janie, and Rachel..." Her eyes had filled with tears. "Well, I just don't know what would have happened to me."

By the time they left Rachel's, Cheryl felt more strongly than ever that God had led her to Sugarcreek.

A little after nine, the front door opened and the Vogel brothers walked in.

"Good morning, Cheryl," Ben called out. "Betsy tells me you have asked her to bring in some of her crafts this afternoon?"

"Yes, I did," Cheryl said with a smile. "I want to begin offering them right away."

"She is very grateful for your help," Rueben said quietly. "And so am I."

Since Rueben rarely spoke to her, Cheryl was touched by his comment. "Thank you, Rueben. She's very talented. I'm blessed to have her work in my shop."

Cheryl realized she'd just called the Swiss Miss her shop. It was the first time those words had slipped out of her mouth. Frankly, it felt good. She smiled as she started the fire in the potbellied stove so the brothers would stay warm as they played checkers. Beau happily curled up under the table, and Cheryl went back to the counter, ready for another day. A few minutes later, Lydia came in. Cheryl noticed she was back to wearing her usual Amish clothing. A long, plain dress and a prayer covering. She wore no makeup, and her hair was back in its customary bun. Cheryl wondered if it meant anything, but she was pretty sure Lydia's involvement in rumspringa wasn't over.

Lydia caught Cheryl watching her. "Just felt like dressing this way today," she said. "I have not made any decisions about the church."

Cheryl just smiled and nodded. She'd asked Lydia to come in early to straighten up the shelves. Saturday's customers had left things in a mess, and with everything going on over the weekend, Cheryl hadn't found the time to put things in order.

Lydia started working while Cheryl added change to the cash register and put on a pot of coffee. She was working on a consignment agreement for Betsy when Lydia came up to the counter.

"I found something else that does not belong," she said.

Cheryl sighed. Had she missed something? Surely Ben was done putting Betsy's crafts on her shelves. She looked up from her paperwork to see Lydia holding a yellow envelope.

"Wh...where did you find that?" she asked.

Lydia pointed toward a shelf full of hand-woven baskets. "Someone bought a basket on top of a stack, and this was inside the next one." She turned it over. "It has your name on it. I hope it is not another scary letter."

Cheryl laughed. "No, it's not scary. I think my aunt hid some letters before she left. We may actually find more."

Lydia smiled. "That sounds like Mitzi. She was always so kind to me. I miss her." With that, Lydia turned and went back to work.

Cheryl stared at the envelope. Did Lydia feel the same way about her? Could she be more supportive? More loving? More like her aunt? "Big shoes to fill," she whispered. "But I'll try to do better."

Cheryl took the envelope and went back to her office. She opened the envelope and took out the letter.

She smiled as she read:

My dearest niece,

   If I have planned this correctly, you have been work-ing at the Swiss Miss for at least a couple of weeks—maybe even a month. I placed this letter inside the baskets because they don't sell as quickly as some of the other items in our store. I hope my timing was about right.

I prayed about what to say to you now that you have been in town for a while without me. I am certain you have made friends because you are very special and people are drawn to you. I know your heart was broken when you came to Sugarcreek, but I pray that you see now that God is in the business of mending hearts. In fact, He can even change them completely! Isn't He wonderful?

I am rather sure that you have begun to compare your life in Columbus to your life in Sugarcreek. That's perfectly normal. In fact, it's healthy. Sometimes we can't see our lives clearly until we step out of our comfort zones. At first, change can be scary, but many times we end up discovering something about ourselves we never knew. I'm guessing you've already learned some wonderful new things about yourself. Perhaps your time in Sugarcreek will lead you back to Columbus. And maybe it will show you that you are happier with the kind of life you're living now. I won't try to sway you either way. That is between you and God. But never be afraid of a new path, my darling girl. God will watch over you. He will never allow you to get lost.

We are both experiencing change, and in my heart, I feel when we are together again, we will both be amazed by the people we've become.

I am so proud of you, honey. Continue to be brave. Continue to try new things. And don't look back. Remember what the Apostle Paul said: "But one thing I do: Forgetting what is behind, and straining toward what is ahead" (Philippians 3:13 NIV).

Keep your focus on the lovely surprises God has waiting. I believe there are amazing things in store for you!

I love you.

Mitzi

Once again, her aunt had given her the right message at the perfect time. Cheryl folded the letter and put it in the drawer of her desk. Then she got up and went out into the shop. As she gazed around at the Swiss Miss, she realized Aunt Mitzi was right. Her life had changed in ways she never saw coming. She was overwhelmed with gratitude to God for the new thing He was doing. Columbus seemed so far away now. And thankfully, so did Lance. For the first time in a long time, Cheryl felt content. She looked forward to her future in Sugarcreek. She had no idea what would come next, but whatever it was, she and God would face it together.

Cheryl looked down when she felt Beau rub up against her leg. "I think we're going to be just fine, you silly old cat," she said softly.

He meowed his agreement, and Cheryl laughed. Then she prepared herself for another day of living and working among the residents of Sugarcreek.

Author Letter

Dear Reader,

After writing six Mennonite-themed novels and seven cozy mysteries, I felt prepared to write an Amish cozy for Guideposts. However, I quickly learned that the world of the Amish is unique. Learning about these gentle people took some effort. But discovering the Amish, who strive to simplify existence down to the basics while honoring their *Gott*, taught me that it takes patience and humility to even scratch the surface of their beliefs. Although most of us would not choose to live as the Amish, we can certainly agree that tuning out some of the noise and distractions of our modern world is an attractive concept. The Amish lifestyle has spoken to me in several ways, and I am richer for getting a glimpse into it. Through Cheryl Cooper's eyes, I was able to experience this unique world from a brand-new perspective. As she tries to understand their traditions, I hope, along with me, you'll begin to appreciate their exceptional way of life.

I am so excited to be working with several wonderful authors who have poured their talents and expertise into this endeavor. Just as importantly, we're blessed to be partnered with Susan Downs and her incredible team of editors whose efforts brought this series to life. With their talented assistance, I believe you'll not only adore Sugarcreek, Ohio, but you'll also fall in love with all the great characters who shape our stories.

Thank you so much for joining us on this journey. As the Amish say, "Today, read a sound book, think a good thought, live a blessed life." We hope this series, Sugarcreek Amish Mysteries, will be full of good books, good thoughts, and lots of special things that will bless you abundantly.

Gott segen eich (God bless you),
Nancy Mehl

About the Author

Nancy Mehl lives in Missouri with her husband, Norman, and their very active puggle, Watson. Nancy has authored twenty books and just finished a romantic suspense series.

She won the Carol Award for mystery in 2009 and has been nominated for two RT Editor's Choice Awards.

Readers can learn more about Nancy through her Web site nancymehl.com. She, along with several other popular suspense authors, is part of the Suspense Sisters (suspensesisters.blogspot.com).

Fun Fact about the Amish or Sugarcreek, Ohio

Although I'd been introduced to the Amish through several wonderful authors, I didn't know much about our setting, Sugarcreek, Ohio. Research revealed an incredibly unique town that has become a popular tourist attraction. Known as the Little Switzerland of Ohio, Sugarcreek was originally called Shanesville after Abraham Shane settled there in 1814. Because its location and climate reminded them of home, the town became a final destination for many German and Swiss settlers. Sugarcreek now has over four thousand residents and is made up of a rich blend of Swiss culture and Amish heritage.

Sugarcreek is full of Amish attractions. Stores like our Swiss Miss Gifts and Sundries Shop are found along Main Street and other locations. These businesses showcase Amish food, furniture, and craft items. During the yearly Swiss Festival, you can experience all sorts of Swiss and Amish traditions.

As you delve into Sugarcreek Amish Mysteries, you'll find some real locations like the Honey Bee Café on Main Street and other fictional businesses we've crafted to resemble real places. For examples, Mrs. Yoder's Kitchen became Yoder's Corner and the Gospel Shop bookstore was turned into By His Grace.

Even though we've taken some artistic license with Sugarcreek, Ohio we pray we've captured the spirit and charm of this wonderful setting. We also hope that as you enjoy your trip to this town, you'll become enamored with Cheryl Cooper, Naomi and Seth Miller, Aunt Mitzi, the Vogel brothers, and other unique and appealing characters. They're all waiting to meet you between the pages of Sugarcreek Amish Mysteries.

Read on for a sneak peek of another exciting book
in the series Sugarcreek Amish Mysteries!

Where Hope Dwells
by Elizabeth Ludwig

The bell above the door to the Swiss Miss chimed a greeting. Cheryl Cooper looked up from the basket she was stuffing and peeked around the long wooden counter that stretched across the back of her aunt Mitzi's gifts and sundries shop. Business had hit a lull in this awkward period between Halloween and Thanksgiving, but with Christmas around the corner, it wouldn't be long before customers once again packed the aisles.

Cheryl straightened and pasted on a bright smile for the flustered-looking woman hovering near the entrance. "Good morning. Can I help you find something?"

The woman flicked a glance in her direction then turned an almost desperate stare on the pull toys on display near the window. "What can you tell me about these?"

Swiping her hands briskly against her jeans, Cheryl rounded the counter and went to stand next to her customer. "Those are all made by local craftsmen. Some of the designs have been handed down for generations. This one, for example"—she lifted a small horse on wheels from the shelf—"was passed down by

Jacob Hoffman's grandfather. Jacob owns the furniture store across the street—"

"How much?"

Cheryl blinked. "I'm sorry?"

The corner of the woman's mouth twitched. "How much for that one?"

"Well, I..."

Cheryl tore her gaze from the woman's thin lips and fumbled for the price tag, but the woman grasped it before Cheryl could, flipped it over, then pulled two twenty dollar bills from her wallet.

"Keep the change."

Cheryl motioned toward the old cash register on the counter where she'd been working. "Are you sure? It'll only take a moment. I can get you a bag."

The bell tinkled again, and this time Naomi Miller, a slender woman in a brown cape dress, stepped through the entrance. She carried a wooden lug crammed with jars of jam.

Cheryl spared a quick smile. "Hi, Naomi. I'll be with you in a moment."

Naomi Miller, Cheryl's friend and mystery-solving partner, shook her head. "No rush. Do you need me to get anything ready for you to take to the farm?"

"Nope. I've got it all together. It's over there on the counter." Cheryl returned her gaze to the woman. "As I was saying..."

But the woman was already stuffing the toy into a large pewter-colored purse with initials emblazoned across its front. "I don't need a bag. Thank you."

She hurried to the door before Cheryl could protest.

A frown bunched Naomi's brow as she too watched the woman scurry away. "What was that all about?"

A feeling of unease pressed on Cheryl's chest as she watched the woman scuttle down the sidewalk and out of sight. She shrugged and turned from the window. "Tourists. Who knows?"

Chuckling, Naomi followed her to the back of the store. "Sorry I'm so late." She lifted the lug. "A few of these jars looked dusty, and I decided to wash them before I put them on the shelves."

At the sound of her cheerful voice, Cheryl's Siamese cat, Beau, leapt from his spot on the counter to weave figure eights around Naomi's feet.

She set down the jams and bent to tickle his chin. "Looks like someone is happy to see me. I guess your maam finally let you come to work?"

"I didn't want to leave him cooped up in the cottage. And yes, he's always happy to see you. So am I." Cheryl smiled and turned the basket on the counter so Naomi could see it. Festooned with blue bows and a card that read *Congratulations* in neat, curvy script, she said, "What do you think?"

Naomi fingered the slender strips of satin. "Is this ribbon new?"

"Just got it yesterday." Cheryl reached under the counter for two handmade baby rattles, one shaped like a fish, the other a bird, and tucked them into the raffia lining the bottom of the basket. "With all the babies being born around Sugarcreek, I had to set these aside." She stepped back and eyed the basket critically. "Well?"

"Very nice." Naomi nodded approvingly then lifted the strap of a floppy tote from around her neck and laid it on the counter. Folding open the flap, she removed two baby quilts. One featured a traditional log cabin pattern, the other, six blocks, a playful figure embroidered in each block.

Cheryl gasped and smoothed her palm over the quilts. "Oh, Naomi."

"I thought you would like them."

"I love them, and so will the Swartzentrubers. They're beautiful." Struck with a thought, she frowned. "You don't think this gift is too extravagant?"

Naomi's gentle smile warmed Cheryl's heart. "Not at all. The family will be blessed by your thoughtfulness."

Cheryl shook her head and tucked the blankets next to the rattles. "You did all the work. I just provided the cloth."

"Do not make light of your contribution, Cheryl. Generosity, in itself, is a gift. You administer yours faithfully."

Though Naomi was shorter by nearly four inches, Cheryl had learned to look up to her friend. Certain her cheeks were as red as her hair, she tucked a stray lock behind her ear then gave the basket a final pat. "Okay, then, I guess it's ready. Sure you don't want to come with me?"

"Ja, I'm sure." A shadow flitted over Naomi's face, and she lowered her gaze. "When Esther gets here to tend the store, I thought I'd pay a visit to Rebecca Zook."

Silence descended at the mention of the grieving mother, so recently made childless.

"Besides," Naomi said, her tone brightening, "I need to get these jars on the shelves. They're all I have left from last summer's strawberry crop." She gestured toward a vacant spot. "I also brought a few more jars of apple butter and the last of my pumpkin butter. Hopefully, there's enough left to last until spring."

As popular as Naomi's jams were with the customers, Cheryl didn't doubt it would be close. She smiled mischievously. "Still no hope of wrangling the recipes from you, I suppose?"

Naomi wrinkled her nose and tugged on the strings dangling from her bonnet.

Cheryl laughed. Hooking one arm through the basket, she said, "All right, then. Thanks again for watching the shop. Please tell Esther I'll see her this afternoon."

Purring loudly, Beau rubbed against Naomi's stockinged leg.

"What about him?" Naomi bent to pick him up. Cradled in her arms, Beau peered at Cheryl through narrowed lids.

She sighed. "You're right. I'll have to run him home first." Fortunately, it was only four blocks and the mild fall weather made the trip pleasant.

"Or I could take him," Naomi offered, tickling Beau's chin and earning another loud purr.

"You don't mind?"

She clucked gently and shooed Cheryl with a wave of her hand. "Go on, now. Tell the Swartzentrubers hello and let them know I'll come around to check on them next week."

"Will do. I know they'll be very glad to see you."

Though no longer a stranger, Cheryl was still amazed by the closeness of the Amish community at Sugarcreek. Their concern and care for one another was a far cry from the harried lifestyle she'd left behind in Columbus. She'd lived there almost six years, yet had never met her neighbors. Here, everyone knew everyone else.

She drew in a lung full of crisp country air as she left the store and hurried to the used Ford Focus she'd driven to work in lieu of her normal walk. She grimaced as she folded herself into the driver's seat, the top of her jeans pinching into her waist. So much for shedding a few pounds. Naomi's cooking had nipped that idea, but quick. She determined to get in some exercise after she left the Swartzentruber's.

Pushing aside thoughts of a diet, Cheryl concentrated on the short drive. The dairy farm wasn't hard to find now that she'd acclimated to the landscape. The first couple of weeks had been a nightmare of new roads and obscure landmarks. Now she felt right at home among the lush hills and farms of Tuscarawas County in eastern Ohio.

A dog's bark greeted her as she pulled into the Swartzentrubers' driveway. Though gruff, she'd learned not to fear old Rufus's warning. A simple dog biscuit could quiet him in a hurry. Smiling, she withdrew a treat she'd tucked into a side pocket of her purse and tossed it over the fence to him before making her way up the stone path to the front door. Rachel Swartzentruber welcomed her after the first knock.

"*Guder mariye*, Cheryl. You are out and about early today."

Like herself, Rachel was an outsider to the Amish community, having only recently joined the church. But she was trying hard to adopt all of their ways, including a few of the Pennsylvania Dutch words and phrases her husband used.

"Good morning, Rachel."

Cheryl accepted a brief hug before being ushered inside. It was nice no longer being the outsider. Sometime during last month's mystery of forbidding notes and strange additions to the Swiss Miss's inventory, she'd become accepted by the community. Many of the families had already dropped the formality with which they treated most Englishers. A few others were still warming to her, but she felt like she was among friends.

"The twins are sleeping," Rachel said, sighing wearily. "I just got them settled and was about to sit down for some coffee. Would you like some?"

Since she hadn't taken time for her ritual caffeine, a steaming cup of black coffee sounded wonderful. Cheryl nodded and followed Rachel into the quaint, farmhouse kitchen.

"The boys still having colic trouble?" she asked, pulling a chair out from the massive oak table that dominated the space.

Rachel nodded and poured two cups from a blue enamelware percolator then carried them to the table. Cheryl missed the morning frappe stops on her way to work back when she lived in Columbus, but she had to admit, fresh coffee brewed over a propane stove was a delicacy she was learning to enjoy just as much.

"I wish I knew what was causing the stomachaches," Rachel continued. Worried lines marred her brow. "Joseph especially suffers from cramps. He keeps us all awake at night."

Which explained the dark circles below her eyes. Cheryl nodded sympathetically, accepted one of the mugs, and took a cautious sip.

Rachel sat then gestured to the basket at Cheryl's feet. "What is that you have brought with you?"

"A gift." Cheryl set her cup aside and lifted the basket for her to see. "It's from Naomi and me. I hope you like it."

Rachel accepted the basket with a sincere thank-you. "They are beautiful," she said, fingering the stitched edges on the log cabin blanket. "That Naomi Miller is quite the seamstress. I only wish I could sew half as well. I simply haven't mastered the patience required."

Cheryl pointed to the dark blue curtains draped above the kitchen sink. "It appears you're learning. Those are new, aren't they?"

Happiness flushed Rachel's cheeks. "They are not so complicated as Naomi's blankets, but I am pleased with the way they have turned out."

"They're sweet," Cheryl said and patted her hand encouragingly. Rachel was a new wife and mother, and everything she did displayed how important it was to her that she make the farmhouse feel like home. Cheryl had felt the same way once...long ago when she'd almost been a bride.

She squelched the thought—and the bitter feelings that accompanied it—and turned her attentions to Naomi's thirty-year-old stepson, Levi. Before coming to Sugarcreek, Cheryl would never have believed she'd entertain romantic notions again—and for an Amish man, no less! Could there be a more different way of life? Yet Rachel and Samuel had found a way to make it work.

Rufus's bark drifting from the front yard cut short her thoughts. Cheryl quirked an eyebrow. "Were you expecting someone else?"

Rachel shook her head. She started to rise, but the dog quickly fell silent. She grimaced and returned to her chair. "Must have been a squirrel. I just hope he doesn't wake the boys."

No sound carried from the nursery, so the two women resumed chatting. Before long, an hour had slipped by. The coffeepot was empty and so was Cheryl's cup. She smiled and rose to leave.

"I know you're busy. I won't keep you any longer, Rachel."

"Thank you for the visit," she replied, standing with her. "It was nice to enjoy some adult conversation for a change."

Cheryl hesitated by the door. "Still no word from your family, I take it?"

A fleeting look of sorrow crossed Rachel's features, and she shook her head. Though they'd been born and raised in Tuscarawas County, her mother and father had not approved of her decision join the Amish community and rarely visited. No doubt, choosing to leave the life she'd known had been difficult for Rachel. Heat warmed Cheryl's face. Was the right man incentive enough to try?

She squeezed Rachel's shoulder. "They'll come around, especially now that they have two fine grandsons."

Rachel ducked her head. "I pray you are right. Samuel doesn't say so, but it hurts him that my parents are so unaccepting."

A crimp gripped Cheryl's heart. She'd been wary of the Amish lifestyle herself, and not so long ago. Ignorance could be a crippling thing.

"Keep praying for them," she whispered. "God will speak to their hearts."

Tears filled Rachel's eyes, but she nodded and opened her mouth to speak. Her words were curtailed by an infant's angry wail. Using a corner of her apron to dab at her red eyes, she managed a watery smile.

"There's Joseph, right on cue. Will you excuse me, Cheryl? I'll get him for you if you'd like to take a peek before you go."

She laughed and motioned toward the hall leading off of the kitchen. "Better hurry or we'll have two squalling babies on our hands."

Rachel's head bobbed in agreement. "That is true. It doesn't take Joseph long to get John riled up. I'll be right back."

Her rubber-soled shoes made barely a sound against the hardwood floor. Cheryl waited patiently, the soft ticking of the mantle clock in the family room marking the seconds. It was certainly a quiet life the Amish lived, with no hum of electricity to fill the air, no squawking television to interrupt conversation or divert attention. A gust from the half-open window riffled the curtains, and Cheryl realized she had even learned to appreciate the whisper of a gentle breeze—something she'd never taken time to notice in Columbus.

"John?"

Rachel's voice carried from the nursery, a surprising note of urgency adding sharpness to her tone. In the background, Joseph continued to wail.

Cheryl furrowed her brow. "Rachel? Is everything all right?" When she received no answer, she took a hesitant step toward the hall. "Rachel?"

"John!"

A second later, the peace Cheryl had been appreciating was shattered by a mother's frantic scream.

A Note from the Editors

We hope you enjoy Sugarcreek Amish Mysteries, created by the Books and Inspirational Media Division of Guideposts, a nonprofit organization that touches millions of lives every day through products and services that inspire, encourage, help you grow in your faith, and celebrate God's love in every aspect of your daily life.

Thank you for making a difference with your purchase of this book, which helps fund our many outreach programs to military personnel, prisons, hospitals, nursing homes, and educational institutions. To learn more, visit GuidepostsFoundation.org.

We also maintain many useful and uplifting online resources. Visit Guideposts.org to read true stories of hope and inspiration, access OurPrayer network, sign up for free newsletters, download free e-books, join our Facebook community, and follow our stimulating blogs.

To learn about other Guideposts publications, including the best-selling devotional *Daily Guideposts*, go to ShopGuideposts .org, call (800) 932-2145, or write to Guideposts, PO Box 5815, Harlan, Iowa 51593.

Sign up for the
Guideposts Fiction Newsletter
and stay up-to-date on the fiction you love!

You'll get sneak peeks of new releases, recommendations from other Guideposts readers, and special offers just for you . . .

And it's FREE!

Just go to Guideposts.org/newsletters today to sign up.

Visit ShopGuideposts.org
or call (800) 932-2145

Find more inspiring fiction in these best-loved Guideposts series

Secrets of the Blue Hill Library
Enjoy the tingle of suspense and the joy of coming home when Anne Gibson turns her late aunt's Victorian mansion into a library and uncovers hidden secrets.

Miracles of Marble Cove
Follow four women who are drawn together to face life's challenges, support one another in faith, and experience God's amazing grace as they encounter mysterious events in the small town of Marble Cove.

Secrets of Mary's Bookshop
Delve into a cozy mystery where Mary, the owner of Mary's Mystery Bookshop, finds herself using sleuthing skills that she didn't realize she had. There are quirky characters and lots of unexpected twists and turns.

Patchwork Mysteries
Discover that life's little mysteries often have a common thread in a series where every novel contains an intriguing mystery centered around a quilt located in a beautiful New England town.

Mysteries of Silver Peak
Escape to the historic mining town of Silver Peak, Colorado, and discover how one woman's love of antiques helps her solve mysteries buried deep in the town's checkered past.

**To learn more about these books,
visit ShopGuideposts.org**